MANOR ZOO

JAMES MICHAEL

Dedication

To George Orwell,
whose *Animal Farm* gave the world a warning that still echoes—
and whose work continues to challenge readers to examine power, responsibility, and truth.

And to the Orwell Estate,
with sincere gratitude for their support and permission to allow this story to exist in conversation with Orwell's legacy. Your stewardship of his work made it possible for *Manor Zoo* to ask new questions while honoring the spirit of the original.

Prologue:
May 2nd, 2020

Beeeeeeeeeeeeep. The sound of the machines woke up Noah, who had fallen asleep holding his wife's hand as he had the last few nights since she was admitted to the hospital with COVID. Noah had known that this day was coming, but he had held out hope that his wife's case would be the miracle that everyone had been hoping for.

"Honey? Oh, sweetheart."

He started sobbing with his forehead on the hand that he still held firmly.

"Don't leave me here. I don't want to be without you, Darling. Please come back to me."

Beeeeeeeeeeeeep

Then, there was a raspy gurgling sound.

A couple of nurses and doctors entered the room in hazmat suits.

"Sir," one of the nurses spoke, "I'm so sorry for your loss, but sadly, we must escort you out so that we can dispose—"

"No! Wait! She just made a sound. I think you can still save her. You have to try!"

"I'm sorry, sir. She is gone. There is nothing left for us to do. We need to get you out of here so that we can—"

"Just," Noah cut her off. He was trying to control his panic. "I'm sorry, but just give me a minute." He turned to his wife who laid there, motionless. He leaned forward and kissed her on the forehead. "I love you, my dear. Save a seat for me."

With her hand still held firmly he reached up with his other hand to move a strand of hair behind her ear. As he did, his wife's eyes shot open. Again he heard the gurgle but it grew into a wretch as she lurched forward. He thought she was vomiting, but as her head raised from the pillow, her mouth opened and her teeth claimed a portion of Noah's forearm just below the elbow. Noah screamed and pulled his arm away.

"Honey, it's me! It's Noah!"

Before she had any chance to respond, her body slumped and she fell back onto the pillow, and Noah saw that the nurse had just injected something into her IV.

"What did you do?" Noah screamed at the nurse.

"Sir, you need to come with us. You have been bitten and we need to check you out."

"I'm fine. Now, save my wife!"

The nurse pointed to the monitor that was still showing no heartbeat.

"I know this is confusing, sir, but this is not your wife. She is gone. What you just experienced is a new mutation of the virus. So please come with us—"

"No! If you can't help my wife, then you can't help me!"

Noah took off. He ran out of the hospital room and down the hall as fast as he could. He heard the hospital staff and then security chasing after him. He started to press the elevator button, but the footsteps were getting louder, so he ducked into the stairwell and raced down the steps the couple of floors to ground level where he found a door to the lobby and another to the parking garage.

Everything felt like it was closing in around him. He quickly burst through the door into the parking garage. At first, he was just grateful to breathe fresh air, but then he realized that the hospital staff and security weren't chasing him anymore. He looked around and noticed how empty the city felt. He started walking home.

It was just over a two mile walk to the Adee Tower Apartments, but as he turned north, leaving the empty Pelham Parkway, he saw a group of people standing outside an apartment complex. There was something strange about the group. They all seemed to be sleeping.

Not sleeping, he thought, *but not awake.*

As he got a little closer, fully content to simply ignore them as he passed, he heard them making the same sounds that he had heard from his wife earlier. About the time that it occurred to Noah that these people could be dangerous is about the time that one of the strangers in the group looked up and saw him. Noah froze. The group all looked up at him and their gurgles changed to a kind of growl and they started limping his direction. Noah immediately turned and ran.

Part 1: The Fall

April 12th, 2020

It was so loud it was hard to understand anything that the director was saying, but the message was clear. The zoo was going to be abandoned. They gave lots of passionate speeches lamenting leaving a place that meant so much to them, but they did their best to avoid saying the quiet part out loud.

The leadership expected all of its employees that had dedicated their lives to caring for the animals to leave them to die in their enclosures.

The director stood at the top of the steps of Astor Court. He was an older gentleman that despite his larger stature appeared frail and beaten down. He did his best to appear stoic and resolute. None of this was his decision, and the beads of sweat that sat on his brow on this cool spring morning betrayed his emotionless demeanor. He had given as much of himself to the zoo, to the animals, as anyone had.

"Listen, everyone, I am upset just like all of you, but I think we all recognize that this is something that simply can't be sustained under the current conditions. COVID-19 has messed up a lot, and our leadership waited too long to handle this in any better way. You all are like family to me. This place feels like home. But the world that existed a year ago is gone. So go home. Hug your loved ones. Take care of yourselves. I love you all."

With that, he descended the steps and cut through the crowd, consciously spaced at least six feet from one another. As he passed, his now former employees shouted different things at him. They shouted their fears for the future. They shouted blame at him for the anxiety they would be living with. The director was visibly affected by their cries.

As he made his way into the zoo center, he quickly heard the door open and close again behind him.

"Please, I have nothing left to say. I'm sorry. Just go home," he said, hoping to avoid more guilt being loaded onto his shoulders.

"Mwen la," a Haitian voice spoke. "I'm here."

The director turned to see his head zoo keeper, Nadege. She was a tall slender woman about the height of the director. She was dressed in her uniform, cargo khaki pants with a navy pullover. Her eyes shone with compassion as they always did. The director let his shoulders relax. If it had been anyone else, he might have ran, but she had always provided a sense of comfort for him.

Morning light filtered through the iron lattice of the Bronx Zoo's front gates, catching on the mist that rose from the fountains and hanging gardens just inside. The city beyond the walls was already awake—sirens, traffic, voices—but here the sound softened, as if the zoo absorbed it and breathed it out more gently.

Nadege stood just past the entrance, hands folded around the strap of her canvas bag, trying not to stare too openly. She had grown up around animals—goats wandering dusty roads, chickens scratching at packed earth—but this was something else entirely. Stone pathways curved away beneath arching trees. Enclosures opened like small worlds stitched together: rock and water and grass arranged with care, not to imitate the wild perfectly, but to honor it.

"No one ever expects it to feel like this," Noah said, smiling as he noticed her hesitation. He was a tall man with a voice that carried the practiced calm of someone used to explaining difficult things to donors, staff, and himself. "They expect cages. Concrete. Signs telling you what you're looking at."

He gestured for her to walk with him.

They moved past the sea lion pool first. The water was impossibly blue, the surface broken by sleek bodies cutting through it like living commas. A young sea lion hauled itself onto a sun-warmed rock and barked, the sound echoing off the stone walls.

"When I started here," Noah continued, "the focus was ticket sales. Always ticket sales. How many people came through the gates, how long they stayed, what they bought on the way out." He shook his head. "Animals were... assets. Attractions."

Nadege frowned. "But they are alive."

"Exactly." He stopped near the railing, resting his hands on the cool metal. "That's the part that gets forgotten."

They walked on. The path narrowed and dipped slightly as they entered a shaded corridor of trees. The smell changed—less water, more earth. Damp leaves. Hay. Somewhere nearby, something large shifted its weight with a low, patient sound.

The elephant habitat opened before them, expansive and quiet. Massive bodies moved slowly through the space, gray skin wrinkled like ancient maps. One elephant lifted its trunk, curling it with deliberate grace to pluck branches from a feeder suspended high above the ground.

"They remember," Noah said softly. "Not in words, maybe. But in routines. In how they're treated. If we're rushed, they know. If we're careless, they feel it."

Nadege watched as a calf pressed close to an older elephant, their sides touching, their steps matched.

"In Haiti," she said, "my grandmother used to say that care is a kind of debt. When something depends on you, you owe it your best."

Noah glanced at her, surprised, then nodded. "That's... actually very close to how I see it."

They continued toward the primate house. The air grew warmer, thicker. Glass panels revealed flashes of movement—hands grasping ropes, eyes watching from shadowed corners. An orangutan sat near the glass, long arms folded loosely, gaze calm and unsettlingly thoughtful.

"These animals didn't ask to be here," Noah said, slowing his pace. "So while they are depending on us, we should do everything we can for them."

He said it plainly, without drama, as if stating a rule as obvious as gravity.

Nadege felt something settle in her chest at the words. Not excitement. Not relief. Something steadier. Like recognition.

They passed the big cats next. Sunlight spilled over artificial rock formations, warming the stone where lions lay stretched out, tails flicking lazily. The smell of raw meat lingered faintly in the air. A tiger paced the perimeter of its enclosure, muscles rolling beneath striped fur, each step measured, controlled.

"When we focus on taking care of them first," Noah went on, "really taking care of them—enrichment, space, respect—they're healthier. Happier. People feel that when they come here. They stay longer. They come back. Visitors don't need to be sold wonder. Wonder shows up on its own."

Nadege smiled despite herself.

They emerged into an open plaza where birdsong filled the air. Bright flashes of color darted overhead as parrots and smaller birds moved between perches. One African gray cocked its head, watching them with sharp, curiousity.

Nadege stopped. "He's watching us."

"He watches everyone," Noah said. "He is going to be a father soon. Waiting for eggs to hatch. They're incubating now. Still, he's smarter than most people I've met."

The bird let out a soft, questioning sound.

Noah checked his watch, then straightened. "There's one more person you need to meet before I turn you loose for the day."

"Who?" Nadege asked, though she already sensed the importance in his tone.

"Our lead veterinarian, Dr. Jones–Walker," he said. "If you're going to work here, really work here, you'll want to learn from him."

He gestured down a side path that curved toward the medical wing, where the smells of antiseptic and straw mingled in the air.

"Come on," Noah said. "This is where the philosophy turns into practice."

When she had started at the zoo, nearly thirty years ago now, she had explained that her name meant hope and tenderness, and to his recollection, he had never failed to feel that when she was around. She had been hired as the zoo was starting to transition from the entertainment focused zoos of the twentieth century to the compassionate, preservation, and rehabilitation focused zoos of the new millenium. To the director, she was the living embodiment of that philosophy. To him, she was the heart of the zoo.

"Nadege, I'm sorry, but there is nothing I can do."

"Director, I know this is not your doing. You love this place and these animals every bit as much as I do."

Tears welled in his eyes. He crossed his arms and shook his head in agreement as he bit his lip and turned his gaze toward the ceiling. He knew that if he allowed himself to feel her compassion that he wouldn't be able to maintain his composure.

"You really are the heart of this place, Nadege. I can't thank you enough for all you have done over the years."

"It was my pleasure, Director."

"I'm not the director of anything. Not anymore. Please call me, Noah. I'm sure you won't since I have been asking you to call me Noah for thirty years now, but please, don't call me director. I just can't handle that right now."

"Well, No— Sir, we have to do something."

"There is nothing we can do. The President has everyone on lockdown, which I suppose is a step in the right direction considering how long it took him to even acknowledge that there was a pandemic."

"I understand, but I will not go home and let these animals wait to die. I simply cannot."

"What could you do? I know you would give everything you have for our animals, but we have nothing to give them. Even if you wanted to feed your body to the lions, that leaves thousands and thousands of animals without food. We have no ability to care for them anymore."

"We can't just leave them. It's cruel."

"You think I don't know that? What would you have us do? Mercy killings? Tell you what, I will go get my gun and every bullet I can find, and I will let you go around and put each one of them down. Does that sound good to you? At least they wouldn't suffer, right?"

Nadege looked in his eyes, and although he spoke from frustration, she could see that he seemed to be begging her to do it.

"Could you do that to them, Nadege? Because I have thought about it since the beginning of this pandemic, and I have learned that I am too big of a coward to save any of these animals that I love so much from the suffering that they will undoubtedly face. Even that damned Capuchin, Dexter."

They both chuckled, thinking about that little monkey who had become a bit of a mascot to the staff because he was always causing mischief, but as soon as someone would try to scold him, Dexter would clasp his hands together and lock his elbows then look up at you with an innocent face. The staff would end up giving him a little scratch under the chin and return to their daily tasks.

"Do you know where your keys are, Sir?"

They gave an outright laugh at that question.

"Sir, we have to do something. Maybe I can get enough of the staff together to volunteer, just enough to help keep them all fed."

"Didn't you hear everyone? There wasn't a single one of them out there thinking about the animals. Everyone is too preoccupied with the terror of their situation, of all of our situations. The world is falling apart. You know I care for these animals, but there is nothing that we have to offer them."

"Then I will do it myself. It has been an honor,

Sir. I wish you well."

With that, Nadege put her hand to her chest and bowed to tell the director that she meant every word. She turned and walked back toward Astor Court. Noah watched her and felt his heart, filled with all of the well wishes he had, leave with her.

The pandemic had forced everyone to drastically alter their lives. At first, everyone just had to wear masks and try to distance themselves when in public. Then came the lockdown. Everyone was forced to stay home. Streaming services, online shopping, and social media became the most important resources. Only "essential workers" were permitted to go to work. Up until that meeting, the zoo staff had been considered essential, but the virus had changed. And even though most of the public wasn't aware of where this change would lead, the world's leaders were scared, and they knew that it was time to draw the line. They just hoped they weren't too late.

"Breaking News! This just in. It is being reported that a new mutation of the COVID-19 virus is on the rise, and is considered extremely dangerous. It has a higher transmission rate and mortality rate. It is also being reported that this new strain carries neurological symptoms that are impacting aggression and decision-making. If you start experiencing any symptoms,

you should quarantine yourself while the symptoms are present. As more information develops, we will be sure to share it. Stay safe, and God Bless America."

May 4th, 2020

For three weeks, Nadege slept in fragments — four hours on a good night, less on most. Her body protested constantly, but she refused to listen. The animals needed her, and thinking too long about the impossibility of it all would only waste time she couldn't afford.

So she began her days the way she always had.

She activated the automatic watering systems first, checking pressure valves by hand where she could. Then came food — not the specialized diets the zoo once prided itself on, but emergency pellets measured carefully to stretch as long as possible. It wasn't perfect. It wasn't enough. But it was survival.

Eventually, she made the decision she had been circling for days.

She opened the aviaries first.

Birds burst into the air in startled waves, feathers flashing as instinct reclaimed them. Then came the natives — animals with some chance of surviving beyond the fences. She worked quickly, forcing herself not to linger on those she couldn't free.

Some would die anyway. She knew that. But a chance, however slim, was better than none.

"Not them," said a familiar voice.

Nadege spun her head around but found no one there.

"Don't let them out. They're mean," the voice said again.

"Nej? Is that you?" Nadege called back.

"I'm Nej," the voice replied as an African Gray Parrot glided down and softly landed on Nadege's shoulder. "I'm Nej."

"Nej! Of course it is you. How are you, my sweet boy?" Nadege said, responding with recognition.

"Scared. Don't let the snakes out. They will try to eat me."

"Oh, Nej, these snakes can't get high enough to get to you. I won't release the tree python yet. I wouldn't let anything happen to you."

"Aww," the parrot responded, "Good Mama." Nej gave a short excited whistle with his reply.

Nadege was feeding the rest of the reptiles when Nej became excited.

"Someone is here. Someone is here! Protect me, Mama!"

"Hello? Is someone there?" Nadege asked while giving Nej some comforting pets.

"Nadege? Is that really you? I guess I shouldn't

be surprised. You always did keep your word," the voice said as it neared the zookeeper and her parrot.

Nadege recognized the voice instantly and relaxed. It was the last human voice she had talked to.

"Welcome back, Director. I hope you are here to help. God knows I could use it."

As Noah approached Nadege, she noticed the balmy glisten of his skin. Most of the humidity of the herpetarium had effectively dissipated over the last few weeks, but Nadege had worked to keep the habitats as livable as possible. So the sweat on Noah's eyelids struck Nadege as odd.

"Did you run here, Director? Why are you so sweaty?"

"Well, the roads aren't really open anymore, so I did have to walk. I came from the hospital."

"Oh, are you not feeling well? Do you need me to get you some water?"

Noah waved his hands in protest.

"I'm fine. I'm just here to help. What can I do?"

Nadege had made a strong enough habit of ignoring her thoughts in order to prioritize getting her chores done that she immediately put Noah to work. With his help, they were able to finish with the chores with enough time for Nadege to make a proper soup for both of them to enjoy for dinner.

Noah confessed that he wanted to help her prepare dinner but that he had just felt so drained lately.

"What did the doctor's say? I assume since you aren't in quarantine that you must not have COVID at least? I surely hope I could trust you to not infect me so carelessly while I am trying to protect our animals."

"I wasn't in the hospital for me. My wife... she just..." his voice caught as he tried to struggle through the rest of his sentence.

Nadege could see clearly enough that Noah was struggling. Everyone had lost someone to COVID by this point, but losing someone so close, to be left alone in a world that had become so bleak, that would be devastating no matter the context.

"Oh my, Direct— Noah, I am so sorry. I hope she passed without any pain. How long ago was it?"

"It's been two days since she passed. Or three. I don't know. It's confusing."

"What is confusing? Do you know what day it is?"

"I know what day it is, but when she died... well, when I thought she had died...

I was sitting there, right next to her bed, holding her hand. She had been struggling to breathe for days. Part of me thought she was too stubborn to die. She had started to sound like she was breathing peacefully until..."

Noah told Nadege about his wife, the bite, escaping the hospital, and the group of strangers.

"You ran here? Were they able to follow you?" Nadege asked. The worry in her voice was clear.

"I didn't come straight here. First, I ran and just tried to find anywhere that I could get into. Eventually, I made it to the Bronx Library Center. I was able to go in there and sleep in the stairwell, but I woke up to someone screaming at me to get out and pointing at my arm."

As he said it, he rolled back his right sleeve to show where his wife had bit him. It was a deep red with raised bumps where her teeth had broken the skin.

"Noah, that looks infected. I think you need to go back to the hospital."

"They won't let you in the hospital if you have a bite. They had guards that had guns drawn on me the whole time I tried to get in. That's when I decided I would come here. I figured if I am going to die, I want to die with these animals. They are the last thing in the world that I love. You being here is just icing on the cake," he said with a little smirk, and Nadege took comfort in seeing that he still held on to some of the playfulness that she had always admired.

As they cleaned up dinner and prepared their bunks, Noah thought best to put some walls in between them for her safety. So they arranged a bunk for Noah in the main hall of the Zoo Center so that Nadege could check on him from above periodically in the night. After getting him settled in, Nadege went back to her room upstairs and began her nightly routine. She had finished her stretches and hanging clothes to dry when she was about to give in to her exhaustion. Then Nej spoke up from his nest.

"Someone is here! Someone is here!"

Nadege sat up.

"Noah? Is that you? Is everything okay?"

There was no response. Nadege stood from her bunk and grabbed the flashlight. Nej flew to her shoulder. When she lifted the light, she saw Noah standing at the entrance to the room. He was breathing so heavily that she could hear the phlegm in his throat. She noticed the vacant look of his eyes.

"Noah, is everything okay? How are you feeling?"

No response.

"Director, go back to bed."

A growl flowed from his mouth.

"Nej, go get help."

Nej flew away and as his wings flapped, Nadege swore she also heard some small feet scampering away.

"Director, I need you to go back to your bed. I need to lock the door. I don't want to have to hurt you. If you will go back to your bed, I will bring you another bowl of soup and some medicine."

For a moment, Nadege felt like she had control of the situation. Noah didn't step toward her, and his breathing steadied. She took a step toward him hoping that it would get him to start moving toward his bed, or at least out of the room. When that didn't work, she continued closing the distance between them. She thought that if she appeared confident, like she had with the animals during all her years feeding animals that could kill her in an instant if they wanted, that she could manage to appear as an alpha and keep Noah from seeing her as prey.

She stood only a few feet from Noah and raised her hand to point over his shoulder.

"Go to bed, Noah. If you don't leave this room immediately, I wi—"

As she tried to deliver her directive she was interrupted as Noah quickly turned his head and bit down on her finger. As she screamed, the pressure grew, turning into heat, and as it felt as though her hand would explode, she felt a release and a white hot pain begin to flow from her knuckle.

Nadege pulled her hand back and swung her other around, which sent Noah falling to the ground.

"Noah, stop. If you get up, I will have to kill you. Stay down!"

But Noah wasn't there. Noah had died of a virus not long after Nadege had left him for the night. Now, the silver fog that coated his eyes and the blood that dripped from his mouth reminded her that she was all alone. She wondered if this is how it would end for her. Then she noticed something shimmering near her feet.

Noah had brought his gun. Nadege wondered if he had been using it for protection since leaving his apartment or if he brought it for the animals. Or for her. She quickly picked up the gun and aimed it at Noah. She continued to plead.

"Noah, please stop. Just go. I don't want to hurt you."

His raspy breath sounded as if there was nothing but fluid in his lungs. She knew what she had to do, but with a growing sense of dread, she realized that she wouldn't be able to do it. She tucked the gun in the back of her pants and raised her hands to show that she meant him no harm.

"Noah, if you kill me, our animals will die. They need me!"

"Nadege, these animals need us. They are wild and exotic, but this isn't their home. Everything that they evolved to do is almost useless here. They need us. And we protect those that depend on us."

"Yes, Dr. Walker. I understand."

"Repeat it back to me, Nadege."

"We protect those that depend on us."

"Very good. If you keep that at the front of your mind, you are going to be a great zoo keeper."

"I am thrilled to be learning under your guidance, Dr. Walker. I had heard horror stories of America, that all the good men were gone. I am glad there is at least one of you here."

"Well, I am flattered. I will have to remind my wife when I get home how lucky she is. And please, if you won't call me Daniel, call me Dr. Jones-Walker. My mother worked hard to make the Jones name something to be proud of."

"Yes, Dr. Jones-Walker. I am sure if your mother could see the compassion you show our animals, she would be very proud indeed. I will make it the purpose of my life to protect these animals."

"Well, make sure you take care of yourself too,

Nadege. This job is tough, even with a good heart."

"In my culture, we believe that animals recognize the spirit in us. So if I give myself to protecting and taking care of them, I believe they will take care of me too."

"Well, that's beautiful, and I hope you're right, but I still wouldn't ask Aslan for a ride if you get tired."

"Noah, Director, stop!"

As Nadege screamed this order at the undead director, she took a step backwards only to slip on the pool of blood that had collected on the floor beneath her now four-fingered hand. She stumbled and fell to her back. She tried to stand up, but Noah pounced. She caught his wrists and held back scratches.

He wasn't strong, but he seemed to not be tiring like she was. As the last of her strength faded away, tears filled her eyes. Nadege was scared, but her tears came from regret that she couldn't protect the animals. She knew that once she was dead that there would be nothing stopping Noah or any other infected from overtaking every single animal still trapped in their enclosure. She begged for a miracle.

At first she didn't recognize the sound. She

didn't feel any tremors, but the powerful sound that reverberated through the building reminded her of an earthquake. Then all of a sudden, Noah was no longer on top of her. She sat up and saw Aslan, the zoo's most beloved lion on top of Noah's body, paws pinning Noah's hands to the ground and Noah's head firmly in Aslan's mouth. Aslan gave a mighty pull and the director's head detached as the rest of the body went limp.

"Good kitty, Aslan. Thank you."

Aslan turned toward Nadege and gave another impressive roar. Before Nadege had a chance to reconsider whether this lion was a blessing, Nej, the African Gray Parrot swooped in and landed on Aslan's shoulder.

"Bring help. He help."

"Very good, Nej. But how did you unlock—"

"More help. Had help."

And as if waiting for their cue, in came Ira the raccoon. Ira wasn't a resident of the zoo in any official capacity, but many of the zoo staff had been involved with chasing him away on multiple occasions and had even witnessed him playing with some of the other smaller animals in their enclosures.

A great effort had been put into capturing him or even figuring out how he was getting into and out of enclosures, but the case remained open. They named him Ira after one zookeeper's favorite host on NPR after they had heard the raccoon described as an "NPR" or "Neighborhood Pickpocket Raccoon." Ira was a legend.

Ira stood next to Aslan (although noticeably behind Aslan's peripheral as if he wasn't entirely confident in his own safety next to a lion) and raised his front paws and wiggled his fingers. Nadege returned the hand gesture to Ira.

"Wow. Thank you, Ira."

Then Nadege looked down at her mangled hand. The delight in her animal rescuers left, and her jaw tightened.

"Now, let's get to work. We don't have much time."

May 5th, 2020

Everyone had their job. Nadege gathered supplies and headed to the front gate, Noah's gun tucked in her pants. The small herd pressed against the tall, black, iron gate. The gate could clearly hold the five infected out, but Nadege knew that the numbers would only grow, and whether it would be the smell of the animals or the noises they would make, they would be drawn to the zoo.

When she finished gathering supplies, she heard chimes from a clock tower to the south. She imagined the tall tower on the Bronx County Courthouse. She always enjoyed driving by it after work. Seeing it made her imagine back when it was constructed. She bet that it was such a big and impressive building. It was sweet to see now, nearly a century later, it is just a small building among skyscrapers.

So she let the bells tell her that even if her effort tonight doesn't save every animal, even if it doesn't save a single one, the fact that she will give everything she has to try, that she did something right and something great. Then like a living metaphor of hope, Nej's wings beat as he slowed to perch on his caretaker's shoulder.

"Help is here. Help is here," Nej chirped.

She turned and as a smile crept across her face

she praised, "Good boy."

Nadege knew what her injuries meant. She would be dead soon. From Noah's account, he got bit by his wife about eighteen to twenty-four hours before he attacked her. And she knew that she couldn't do what needed to be done by herself.

"Nej, take Ira and go free all of the animals! You must hurry!"

"Not snakes."

"Nej, *all* animals."

"Not snakes. They're mean."

"Take Aslan. They animals will respect him."

The three animals turned to begin their liberation. Their first stop was the bear complex. As they approached the gate, Mama, a blackbear, the matriarchal alpha of the bears, was there. Ira began working on getting the gate open. Aslan spoke to Mama.

"We are freeing all the animals. Can you help?" His voice was low and mighty.

"I must stay with the cubs, but my son, Mowgli

will go with you, he can help with the locks. Be safe." Mama's voice was sweet with a southern charm that also hinted at a fierceness very near the surface that could be accessed in an instant.

The animals made it to the elephant habitat next.

"Aslan, sir, let me address the herd leader. We know each other from when we were younger. We were both born here. I can help keep things calm." Mowgli's voice was youthful but carried a convincing confidence that promised certainty.

"You have my trust. Be safe." Aslan's fatherly tone and accent gave his approval an almost divine quality that made Mowgli feel slightly bigger than before. Aslan watched at the fork in the path as Mowgli approached the elephant gate. An elephant lowered its trunk over the gate, and Mowgli sat back and hugged the trunk as it wrapped around him. Aslan turned and hoped that his reunion with Ernie would be as warm.

As the lion approached the Gorilla Forest with Ira in tow, Aslan heard something hitting the ground repeatedly. As they passed a lightpost, he realized what it was.

"Careful, Ira," he chuckled. "They're throwing poop."

"Is it for you or for me?" the nasally-voiced raccoon laughed back.

The pair reached the gate where Ernie, the silverback, stood waiting.

"Was the poop really necessary?" Aslan growled.

"Don't know what you're talking about. That's chimp stuff, but I suppose we all look the same to you," Ernie retorted. There was an intense stare between the two beasts. Then Ira broke the silence.

"Aren't both of you guys from Africa?"

The two kept staring until Ernie's lips pulled back and revealed a smile so big that you would forget about the imposing stature of the silverback. Aslan returned the smile with a laugh, and the two embraced as Ira finished getting the gate open.

"It is good to see you, Brother. We are freeing all of the animals. Can you help?" Aslan's question perfectly communicated the affection, respect, and trust that the two leaders shared for each other.

"Not only will we help, we are going to free more animals than you," Ernie's casual yet intimidating voice challenged.

"If this is a race, then Happy and Jwaye's groups are with us," Mowgli said as he caught up with Aslan and Ira. He and the elephant, Happy, had just made it to release the orangutan's habitat to recruit the third member of their nursery brotherhood, Jwaye, an adolescent orangutan who grasped Happy's trunk and held on as he was lifted to ride Happy as the trio turned to secure a headstart.

"Meet you at the front gate. Last one there is a rotten egg!" Jwaye shouted as the three hurried down the path.

As the groups went in different directions, Aslan found satisfaction in the camaraderie that Mowgli was able to create amongst the animals. His next stop was the tiger habitat though, and he was less than confident that they would be as enthusiastic to help.

"Come, Ira. We don't want to let them get too far ahead."

As Aslan approached the tiger habitat, he noted the change. The path narrowed slightly, bending through dense plantings meant to feel accidental—tall grasses, low shrubs, trees spaced just enough to block clean sightlines. The air even smelled different here: damp earth, old leaves, something faintly metallic from the reinforced barriers hidden beneath the greenery.

When they got to the gate, there were multiple tigers waiting rather than just the pack leader as it had been with the other animals. Aslan knew that the culture of the tigers was not that of a community. Tigers were very self-serving animals that never failed to put their own survival above the well-being of the group.

"Listen, please, everyone. The zoo is under attack. We need everyone's help to keep the zoo safe."

There was commotion amongst the tigers, but Aslan got the impression that they were ready to help. It was validating for Aslan to know that even though there were innate urges, that the sense of family seemed to exist throughout the zoo. He had a feeling that Nadege had done a lot to help create that, her and the good doctor. Then one voice spoke up above the other tigers.

"Why should we care? We can take care of ourselves." The voice was silky but sardonic. The tigers looked around for the source, but no one stepped forward to claim the callous comment. Then another tiger near the front of the group spoke up.

"We will help. I have friends outside of this enclosure. Is Happy free?" It was Sarabi, another adolescent that had been cared for in the nursery with Mowgli, Happy, and Jwaye. Aslan again took comfort in the future of his zoo family.

"He is. He is with Mowgli and Jwaye, and we are racing the primates to see who can release the most animals and get to the front gate where Nadege is preparing for our efforts."

"Then we are losing time."

As Sarabi spoke, the gate slid open and Ira scrambled onto Aslan's back seeking cover in his mane. Sarabi led the tigers and they raced down the path toward the front gate.

As Nadege watched the population of the zoo descend upon the front gate, she was filled with hope. Her story's ending had already been written, but her optimism flourished at the sight of all of these animals, that would be fighting in the wild, running side by side toward a common purpose. Nej left her shoulder as Aslan came to a stop at the front of the blended herd, and Nej took his place on Aslan's shoulder.

"Help is here. What now?"

They started by reinforcing the gate. They reinforced the locks by adding chains and cables to provide more stability, keeping the gate closed. The primates helped by gathering rocks and "mud" to stuff into the gate's hinges to prevent the gate from being able to swing at all.

The elephants helped by moving barricades to reinforce parts of the gate and to limit the visibility of outsiders. They broke branches off of trees to stuff into the gate for the same purpose.

"Nej, we want to have a backup plan in case the gate fails. Can you ask Happy to reposition some of the barricades near the weakest point of the gate so that if the gate is penetrated, any visitors will be forced into a bottleneck? This will help keep the defense focused on a small number at a time in the event of a breach."

Nej flew to Happy's head, but before Nej could say anything, Happy pushed a concrete barricade, angling it perpendicular to the gate opening.

"Good boy, Happy. You are so smart," Nadege praised.

"Happy is good, smart boy. Good Happy," echoed Nej.

Happy continued to work, moving the barriers to create a funnel, so if the gate ever opened, the infected would limp their way single file and hopefully allow whatever animals time to deal with them. The animals also created some platforms to allow a watcher to supervise the front gate from a safe location. Once all of the gates were fortified, the animals all gathered back at the front gate where Nadege tried to give all of the animals an idea of what was ahead of them.

"I'm not sure how much you understand me, but the humans have abandoned us. They are infected and dangerous. Keep them out. For nearly thirty years, I have protected you. I have cared for you. I have loved each of you. And you have all depended on me for that care... but..." Her voice caught in her throat, but she steeled herself.

"I won't be here to protect you anymore. I have been infected. So I need you all to protect each other when I am gone. We protect those who depend on us. All of you will now be depending on each other. Protect each other. *Nou pwoteje sa ki depann de nou.* We protect those who depend on us."

As she spoke she wondered whether the animals could understand any of what she said, but when she repeated her and the good doctor's mantra, Aslan gave a mighty roar, and all of the other animals echoed the great lion's sentiments as the zoo walls shook with the pride of a family that was more than what nature could create.

Once the noise settled down, Nadege led the animals as they marched to the Dancing Crane Plaza. There, in the middle of the plaza, was the bunk she had slept in for nearly a month. But it wasn't empty.

After she sent Aslan with Ira and Nej to release the animals, Nadege's attention went to her friend, the last human she would ever see, Noah. She picked up all of his body and put it on the gurney she had been sleeping on for the last three weeks. She wrapped the corpse in her sheet and buckled the body in.

"Let's have one last tour, eh, Director?"

She pushed the gurney down the hall to her friend's old office and opened the door.

"Director. Noah, this is who you are." She walked around his office, to the desk he had sat at for nearly half a century. She picked up a picture he had left on his desk. It was Noah and his wife. They were laying in some grass, and Noah was sneezing while his wife laughed. Nadege smiled as a tear fell from her eye.

"This is you, sir. The love that you and your wife shared is not gone from this world. It did not leave with you. You have left it for the rest of us to enjoy. Thank you for your gift. You were a friend and a good man. I am better for having known you. Thank you for your gift."

She took the photo and brought it to the gurney and placed it on Noah's chest. She wheeled him carefully down the stairs and out of the zoo center to the middle of the Dancing Crane Plaza. Then, she went and got some gas from the emergency generator and poured it on the gurney and the remains of her friend. Then she made a trail with the gas a safe distance from the gurney.

Finally, she took an empty wheelchair and placed it at the feet of her friend. She secured some loose cables to the arms and feet of the chair. She stared at the empty chair that would be her exit from this life and felt a moment of regret. Regret that she hadn't done more. Made a family. She pushed it out of her mind. She had work to do.

Nadege walked up to the gurney and placed her hand on Noah's forehead.

"See you soon, my friend."

Then, she turned and picked up the gas can and gave herself a quick rinse of the gasoline. She took her lighter from her pocket and sat down in the wheelchair. She slipped her feet in and tightened the cables. Then her left arm and tightened it with her right hand. Finally, she took the lighter into her right hand put it through a cable that she was able to tighten with her mouth. Trembling, she opened the lighter.

FLICK

CLINK

She dropped the lighter. She had opened it, but when she tried to flick the igniter, her hand slipped with gas. The lighter hit the floor.

She started to panic. She was in a coffin of her own making, but she no longer had a way to die. She could feel her brain getting fuzzy. She tried to focus. She heard flapping.

Nej glided down to the lighter and picked it up. Nadege reached out with her hand, but Nej flew back to the animals and landed near Ira. Ira opened the lighter and flicked the igniter, and a warm and welcoming glow was a beacon to help Nadege find her way home.

Nej grabbed the lighter and flew to Nadege but stopped at eye level at the end of the trail of gas. Nadege looked at the bird that she had been there when it hatched and had fed it as a baby. She realized that she thought of him almost as a son.

"We are family," Nej said.

"You are mother," he continued. Then he flew closer to her just off center so that he could look into her eyes with one more message for his mother.

"We are better for having known you."

As Nej said those words, all of the animals in the zoo paid their respects to their beloved zoo keeper. Their mother. Some bowed. Others howled or called. Some leaned on each other. Then Nej flew higher, drawing Nadege's gaze toward the heavens, and she smiled as peace swept across her face.

And Nej dropped the lighter.

Part 2: On Our Own

Day 1

The sun rose without ceremony. Its light crept across the stone paths of the zoo, touching ash before fur, smoke before breath. The charred remains of a gurney and wheelchair at Dancing Crane Plaza were cold now—just blackened earth and a faint scent that none of them could name, but all of them felt. They gathered anyway.

Not in a circle. Not at first. They came in drips and starts, keeping distance, watching one another, feeling the instinct that says *be wary* while another part of them, the part that called the zoo home, felt comfort in the presence of family.

Nej landed last.

He settled on the twisted metal of a broken signpost, feathers puffed slightly against the morning chill. His yellow eyes scanned the group—counting, measuring, remembering. Mama sat heavily near the fire pit, head bowed, shoulders hunched forward as if she was shouldering the gravity of the situation on her own.

Happy stood behind her, massive and unmoving, trunk resting against the ground like a column holding the sky in place.

Rocket was already there, of course—half in shadow, half in sun, eyes half-lidded, as though this were only another chapter in a book he'd already finished centuries ago.

Ernie stood apart, knuckles pressed into the dirt, broad back rising and falling with slow, controlled breaths. His gaze never stopped sweeping the paths.

Aslan arrived without sound. He stepped forward, mane catching the light, eyes reflecting it back with something like fire. The others shifted—not fear, but recognition.

And then the tigers came. Not as one body, not as a line—just a loose clustering at the edge of the plaza. Their tails flicked. Their ears turned. Their muscles remained coiled, undecided.

Sarabi stepped ahead of them. She did not bare her teeth. She did not raise her voice. She simply stood—head level, shoulders squared, eyes steady.

The others quieted. For a long moment, no one spoke. Then Nej cleared his throat.

"She said...," he began, then stopped. The words did not come easily, even to him.

Mama lifted her head. Her voice was low and rough.
"Say it," she said. "If you don't, it'll rot inside you."

Nej nodded once.

"She said we must protect those who depend on us."

The words settled over them like ash.

Rocket snorted softly. "A fine sentence," he said. "Comforting. Vague. Humans love those."

Happy shifted his weight, the ground murmuring beneath him. "She lived by it," he said. "That matters."

Rocket's eye opened a fraction more. "So did many who didn't survive."

Aslan's tail flicked once. "Enough," he said calmly. "She died so we could stand here. We don't get to call that meaningless."

Ernie rumbled low in his chest. "There were infected at the gate yesterday," he said. "They'll be back. Meaning won't stop them."

Mama rose to her full height.

"When my cubs cry," she said, "I don't ask whether answering is efficient. I answer." Her gaze swept the group. "We were her cubs."

The tigers stirred. Sarabi stepped forward one pace.

"She fed us," Sarabi said. Her voice was even, measured. "She never flinched. Not when we roared. Not when we bled." Her eyes flicked briefly to the others behind her—an unspoken reminder.

"We will not tear each other apart today," she

continued. "Not while her ashes are still warm."

No challenge followed. No dissent.

Happy inclined his head slightly.

Aslan looked at Sarabi with quiet approval.

Rocket exhaled through his nostrils. "Unity," he muttered. "Temporary, and rare."

Nej tilted his head. "Temporary things still matter," he said.

Ernie shifted closer to the center. "If this is a council," he said, "then say it. And if it is, say what we do next."

Aslan stepped closer to the fire pit, gazing down at the ash. "We stand guard," he said. "We fortify. We do not wait to be hunted."

Mama's voice softened. "And the small ones?"

Aslan met her eyes. "They hide behind us."

Rocket chuckled quietly. "That story ends badly more often than not."

Nej fluttered his wings once. "Only when the strong forget who they're standing for."

Happy traced a line in the dirt with the tip of his trunk. "Then this," he said, "is the beginning. Not of rule. Of responsibility."

Sarabi spoke once more. "Then let it be remembered," she said, "that the tigers stood together when it began." She stepped back. The others followed.

Mama pressed her paw into the dirt beside the ashes.

"For her," she said.

Aslan followed. Then Ernie. Then Happy. After a pause, Rocket scraped forward as well.

Nej watched them all.

"Then we will remember," he said. "And we will decide."

The sun climbed higher.

The zoo did not belong to humans anymore.

But it did not yet belong to monsters, either.

The council heard from all animals that wanted to speak, and a list of all concerns was made and a priority of those concerns. First, the zoo animals all insisted that fortification of the walls was necessary as well as additional improvements to the security.

It was agreed that they should have one gate operational so that if any animals should want to leave or need to escape if the zoo is overrun. Happy volunteered to do the heavy lifting required for that task, but Attenborough the Beaver (AB for short) insisted that he could engineer a door on the front gate so that the funnel could be utilized to clear herds that gathered outside the fence.

"This will be a job that requires finesse more than brute strength," AB chided.

"Well, I will help in whatever way you need," Happy replied, ignoring the beaver's sass.

"We should also look at creating some additional preventative measures outside the walls. If we dug some pits deep enough to keep the infected in them, that could help us keep the pace even more under control," AB added.

Aslan agreed.

"Keeping them contained could also allow us the opportunity to bring in some meat for some of the animals. Good work, AB."

Finally, there were talks to organize a patrol. It was agreed that all adult animals should participate in the patrol. A tiger spoke up in dissent.

"A patrol is a nice idea, but not all animals are able to provide the same level of protection as others. I, for one, don't even have any claws since the humans took them from me."

Aslan thought he recognized the voice from when he had gone with Ernie to open the tiger's habitat.

"That is a good point," Aslan started, "No one should be on patrol alone. What is your name, tiger?"

"The humans called me Chester," he admitted ashamedly. "One of the idiots thought the damned Cheeto mascot was a tiger."

Aslan turned and addressed the council.

"Chester is right. When we are making the patrol schedule, we need to make sure that no one is on patrol by themselves. That way, if one is needed to fight a herd, the other can work to alert the zoo. Chester, I would welcome your brotherhood on patrol. You and I can work together."

Chester feigned a smile as he turned and exited, annoyed.

There is something familiar about Chester, Aslan thought. For the meantime, he let himself confuse familiarity with comfort.

Week 1

The first week was one that left every animal in the zoo feeling like they could accomplish anything. Under AB's oversight, the walls and gates were reinforced, and as promised, AB with his team of beavers that called themselves "Balanced Beaver Calculations" engineered a piece of the iron-bar fencing to attach to a counter-weight and pulley system that would allow the animals to open a small section of the gate, funneling any zombie herd into a single-file line.

Then, AB guided teams of the zoo's best diggers made up of bears, wild dogs, wart hogs, and mongooses to dig a couple of pits every day. They hoped that wandering infected would fall into the pit and be unable to get themselves out. Although Aslan had suggested that the meat would be good to eat, more than a few animals had reservations about the look of the infected and whether they would be willing to eat them.

At the end of the week, Aslan had asked the animals to meet near the front gate. The animals gathered near the gate, the iron still warm from effort, the air heavy with dust and breath. Aslan stood where the light broke against the stone, not above them, but visible to all.

"This place was not saved by teeth," Aslan said. "Nor by strength alone." He let his gaze move slowly across the group—large, small, predator, prey.

"It was saved because we did not act as cages taught us to act. We did not flee when we were afraid. We did not take more than we needed." He paused, tail still, voice steady.

"Some of us lifted. Some of us planned. Some of us watched. Some of us stood where standing mattered. None of it worked alone."

A murmur rippled through the animals—agreement, recognition.

"This gate does not belong to one species," Aslan continued. "It belongs to all who will hold it. And it will only stand as long as we remember why we built it."

Then, softer—but no less firm, "We protect those who depend on us. That is not a promise. It is a responsibility." Aslan lowered his head slightly—not in submission, but in acknowledgment.

From the back, barely audible, Chester muttered sarcastically, more to himself than anyone else, "Long live King Aslan."

A few ears turned. Aslan did not. The gate stood. For now.

As night fell, Aslan went to find Chester to start their patrol.

"Chester, it's time for our patrol. Follow me."

"Right away, my king," Chester said, mocking a bow.

The two walked to the front gate, where their patrol was to be posted.

"Everything looks pretty calm," Aslan said, "How are you feeling?"

"What do you mean? I'm fine, your highness."

"I'm nobody's king. I can just tell that everyone expects me to lead. I think we would all be better off if things were decided on as a group. But I was just asking because I'm still trying to figure out why you were against doing patrol. If I hadn't had to tear one of the infected off Nadege, I would probably be scared of them too."

Chester scoffed. He was insulted by the idea that he was scared.

"I'm not scared. I just don't have the same ability to protect myself as you do, and us tigers don't have that same *family* feeling that you pack animals do. I'm not going to kill myself for these animals."

"I hope no one has to die to keep everyone safe. That's kind of the point of setting up the patrol. So that we aren't surprised by any threats. Having multiple animals on patrol was a good idea though. I wouldn't want anyone to be on their own, especially if they didn't want to be out here in the first place. It would just put everyone at risk."

"You are still at risk. My being here doesn't make you any safer. I won't save you. And those surprise threats never go away. That's what makes them 'surprises.' They always seem to be a lot closer than you think." Chester's tone became more ominous with every menacing word.

Aslan laughed as the two big cats stepped up to the platform over the gate where they could check the pits.

"Looks like the pits are already working," Aslan said, seeing that 4 infected stood motionless in the pit.

"Go strike down your enemy, King, lest your subjects revolt."

"I thought that clearing the pits may be a job better done from a distance. Maybe we burn them, or maybe the elephants and grab them with their trunks so that we can avoid bites and scratches."

"You aren't scared are you, King Aslan?" the biting sarcasm grew with every word that flowed from his fangs.

"Not scared. Patient," Aslan retorted, but he was done sweeping Chester's disrespect under the rug.

"And for whatever it is worth, your secret is safe with me."

"Oh, and what secret is that?"

"You see, when I was a cub, there was an elder in our pride that was desperate to return to his home in the wild. He was so desperate that one day he decided that he would try to run out before the gate closed after a feeding."

"Did he make it?" Chester pretended to take an interest in the story.

"Not even close. He got his paw smashed in the gate. He had to have surgery. During surgery, they had to remove his claws from that paw to allow it to heal properly. I can still see the scars that it left on his paw. They are the same scars that are missing from your paws."

Chester bared his teeth, but Aslan turned with a laugh, not taking the threat seriously.

"Like I said, your secret is safe with me. I don't need you or any other animal to be like me. Whoever you are, I'm glad to have you hear. We are on the same team, and I think our team is better for having you on it."

Chester calmed as he looked past Aslan. Then he raised a paw to point, extending his claw.

"I guess I would have to agree because it looks like the pits aren't deep enough to keep the infected in it afterall."

Aslan turned and saw the four still in the pit, but once was now at the gate as well.

"It looks like they are still in the pit. I think that one by the ga–*agh...*"

Aslan put a paw to his neck as blood began to pour from the tear that Chester's quick hands had just created.

"Oh me, I can be so careless with these silly things. Did I get you, my king?"

As Chester leaned his head toward Aslan's mouth to allow him to whisper, he put a paw on Aslan's shoulder and gave a powerful shove, sending Aslan to the ground, outside of the gate. His body hit the ground at the edge of the pit, but his momentum carried him into the excited herd of infected. Their frenzy was a stark contrast to Chester's demeanor. It wasn't patience. It was practice.

Chester jumped down from the platform and cut the line that held up the vertical gate, leaving a portion completely open. Chester gave the signal to the zoo that there had been a breach. To Chester's surprise, more than just the one zombie appeared at the opening. He turned and ran, screaming that there was an attack on the zoo.

Chester didn't get far before he came across Happy the elephant.

"Happy, thank goodness. Aslan needs our help. We noticed the gate was compromised, and Aslan went to inspect it when a herd surprised him. He sent me to get help."

Before Chester could say another word, Happy rushed to the gate where three infected were staggering down the path. Happy picked up one by the ankles with his powerful trunk and whipped him into the ground. The zombie's head exploded on impact, and Chester pounced on it to rip the arms off the unmoving zombie.

Happy picked up the second in the same fashion and used it as a club to smash the other zombie.

"Where is Aslan?" Happy shouted.

"He must have gone out of the gate to slow the herd."

Happy walked to the gate and could see the frenzy taking place in the pit.

"I've got to get out there! They're killing him!" Happy declared.

"Happy, wait!" Chester said going up to the platform where he had taken the lion's life. He was now eye level with Happy. "He is already lost, Happy...

What a terrible tragedy, but Aslan taught me that it is better to be patient than to rush. Listen. He isn't making a sound. It is too late for Aslan. We must tell the others and get the gate fixed."

Happy stood there in shock. His eyes dropped and he noticed a pool of blood under Chester's paw.

"Are you hurt too, Chester? You're bleeding."

Chester looked down and pretended to be shocked.

"Oh my. I'm fine, Happy. I just seem to have stepped in some blood, but that means..." he put a paw to his mouth, "those creatures must have torn him apart with such ferocity that his blood splattered all the way up here. What an awful end to such a dear, dear friend."

Happy draped his trunk across Chester's shoulders to comfort the poor defenseless tiger.

"Come on, Chester. Let's go tell the others."

As the two animals turned to go deliver the news, there was a loud crash. They turned and found the gate completely on the ground with dozens of infected coming into the zoo. Happy raised his trunk and blew with all his might, the call to all patrol to report.

Nej was the first to arrive, and as soon as he saw the scene, he flew around the entire zoo announcing to all the animals that a breach had occurred at the gate.

Happy grabbed another zombie, and was working to dispatch as many as he could, but they just kept coming. Happy was being surrounded, but luckily, the fingernails of the infected were not enough to break through his tough skin.

Just as Happy was about to consider himself invincible, one of them fell onto his head from the platform, and he realized that his eyes were completely vulnerable. He closed his eyes shut and started swinging his head to try and throw the zombie off. Then, all of a sudden, the zombie was gone, and there was a loud roar.

"Thanks, Chester. That was a little too close," he said as he opened his eyes, but it wasn't Chester.

"Where's Aslan?" screamed Ernie as he smashed his fists down onto the zombie's skull, crushing it in a single blow. Before Happy could give Ernie the news about Aslan, he leapt from the platform and continued attacking the infected. Happy watched as Ernie quickly smashed another zombie.

At first, Happy took it as a challenge and picked up another zombie and swung it through two more before releasing the zombie, sending it flying more than twenty feet into the air before crashing to the ground in a mangled heap. Then, Happy looked beyond Ernie and felt strength well up within him.In the distance, Happy could see what looked to be every animal in the zoo answering the call to fight off the breach.

Mama felt it before she saw it. The ground carried the warning first—a tremor traveling up through her paws and into her chest. Stone scraping stone. Metal shrieking. The sound of the gate being forced, bent where it should not bend.

"Mowgli," she said, already turning. Her son was at her side, taller than he had any right to be, his shoulders no longer cub-round but not yet fully broad. His eyes were bright with fear and something sharper beneath it—resolve.

"No," Mama said, stepping in front of him. Her bulk blocked the path instinctively, the way it always had. "You stay."

"Mama—"

"No." She pressed her forehead to his, breath warm and heavy. "This is not for you."

The roar of the breach echoed again. Something gave way with a sound like tearing bone.

Mowgli swallowed. "Happy's there."

Mama flinched despite herself.

"And Jwaye," he said softly. "He's there too."

She pulled back, searching his face for hesitation, for doubt—anything she could grab onto and hold. There was fear there, yes. But it wasn't the fear of a cub hiding behind his mother anymore. It was the fear of someone who knows exactly what they might lose.

"They need me," Mowgli said. "You taught me that."

Mama's jaw tightened. She had taught him that. She had taught him everything that was now undoing her.

"We protect those who depend on us," he continued, voice shaking but steady enough to stand on. "They depend on me."

"They depend on *me*," Mama growled. "And I depend on you staying alive."

Mowgli shook his head, stepping back before she could reach for him again. "If I stay, and they die... I won't be alive anyway. Not really."

For a heartbeat, the world narrowed to just the two of them—the smell of fur and earth, the memory of winters slept side by side. Mama saw him then not as the cub she had raised, but as the bear he had become. Her son.

She huffed a broken sound from deep in her chest. "Run fast," she said. "And if it turns... if it turns bad—"

"I'll come back," Mowgli said, already moving.

Mama reached out, claws scraping stone where he had been a moment before.

"Come back," she whispered to the empty air.

The gate was a slaughter. Mowgli smelled it before he saw it—rot and blood, fear soaked into fur. Bodies lay scattered where the patrol had met the breach head-on. Too many. Too still.

His paws slowed. His breath hitched. This was wrong. This was too much.

A shattered barricade leaned at an angle it was never meant to hold. Infected pressed through in jerking waves, their bodies breaking against stone and horn and tusk alike. Somewhere ahead, something screamed—a sound high and terrified, not dead.

Mowgli ducbehind a toppled concrete slab, heart hammering so hard it hurt. He crouched low, fur brushing cold ground, trying to make himself small. He wasn't ready. He wasn't—

A crash cut through his thoughts.

"Jwaye!"

The orangutan was backed against the gate's inner frame, one arm uselessly pinned, eyes wide with terror. A zombie lunged, fingers scraping for fur.

Mowgli didn't think. He moved.

The world snapped into focus—muscle and instinct and the echo of Mama's voice inside his chest. He slammed into the first zombie with a roar he didn't recognize as his own, claws tearing through dead flesh that barely noticed pain.

Another came. Then another.

Jwaye screamed as teeth sank into his shoulder, the sound ripping through Mowgli like fire.

"No!" Mowgli surged forward, throwing himself between them, taking the bite meant for his friend. Teeth sank into his neck. Pain flared, hot and blinding.

But Jwaye was free. With a desperate, furious cry, the orangutan brought both fists down on the zombie's skull. Bone shattered. The body dropped.

Mowgli swayed.

The world tilted. Sounds dulled, as if sinking underwater.

Jwaye caught him before he fell. "You did it," Jwaye whispered, voice breaking. "You saved me."

Mowgli's legs buckled. He slumped against his friend, breath shallow, vision darkening at the edges.

"Worth it," he murmured.

Jwaye sobbed, clutching him, blood soaking both of them. "I don't want you to—"

Mowgli smiled faintly, eyes already glazing. "Tell Mama... I ran fast."

His body went heavy. Still.

Jwaye screamed.

Chester watched it all from the shadows.

The chaos gave him cover—the perfect excuse. He slipped along the edge of the breach, eyes sharp, calculating. He would leave. Let the fools die. Let the story write itself.

A soft voice stopped him.

"I saw you."

A female red panda stood atop the fallen barrier, fur singed, eyes bright with shock and fury. "You killed him," she said. "You killed Aslan."

Chester's smile didn't reach his eyes. "Careful," he purred. "This is not the time for accusations."

"It's always the time for the truth," she snapped, stepping closer. "I'm telling the council."

She turned.

Chester moved.

It was quick. Quiet. His claws flashed once, precise and final. Her body fell among the others, small and easily lost in the wreckage.

Chester stepped back, breathing hard. He glanced around, then dragged her closer to the breach, smearing blood and ash where it would tell the right lie.

When he lifted his head again, his voice carried perfectly.

"She didn't make it," he called. "The breach took her."

No one questioned it.

Above the bodies, the gate groaned—holding, for now.

And far from the noise, Mama lifted her head and roared.

Somewhere deep inside, she already knew.

The Aftermath

The fire burned low. Not from lack of fuel—there was plenty of that—but because no one had the heart to feed it yet.

Bodies lay where the battle had ended, shapes half-lit by embers and dawn. The air smelled of ash and iron and something sour that clung to the back of the throat. No one spoke. Even the birds were silent, perched high and watching, feathers tucked tight as if sound itself might wake the dead.

Ernie lay near the gate, massive even in stillness. The silverback's chest bore deep wounds, his great hands curled inward as though he were still holding the line. He had been a wall once. He had not broken.

Mowgli lay closer to the inner path. Jwaye still held his friend. He swayed as strength flowed from his wounds. His eyes barely able to stay open.

Mama found him there.

She did not roar this time. The sound that left her was smaller—an animal sound stripped of all strength, torn loose from somewhere too deep to name. She lowered herself beside him, pressing her forehead to his fur, breathing him in as though warmth might return if she tried hard enough.

His face was peaceful.

"He ran fast," Jwaye whispered.

"Just like I asked."

She stayed there until the sun crested the broken skyline, painting his fur gold one last time. Happy came to take Jwaye to Rocket who had taken charge of caring for the injured. He gave Mama Bear a comforting stroke on her back with his trunk. Then he left.

The infirmary was crowded but quiet.

Rocket moved slowly among the injured, his ancient shell dusted with blood and ash. He worked without commentary, without ceremony. Leaves crushed. Aloe pressed. Wounds cleaned as best they could be.

Jwaye lay on his side, bandaged thickly, breath shallow but steady. His eyes were open—too open—staring at nothing.

"You're alive," Rocket said gruffly, more command than comfort. "Which means you'll need to stay that way."

Jwaye swallowed. "Mowgli—"

"Later," Rocket cut in gently. "Later is for grief. Now is for living."

Jwaye turned his face into the bedding and wept soundlessly.

Tashi did not understand at first.

He moved through the aftermath with quick, uncertain steps, weaving between legs and bodies, his ears flicking at every sound. He called out softly, the way he always did when he couldn't see her.

"Mama?"

No answer.

"Mama?"

He followed a familiar scent toward the outer edge of the grounds, toward a place red pandas should never have been. His steps slowed. His tail drooped.

She lay on her side near the fallen barrier. Her stillness felt heavier than anything Tashi had ever felt.

Tashi nudged her shoulder. Once. Twice.

"Up," he whispered. "We have to go back."

She did not move.

The world seemed to tilt, as though the ground itself had betrayed him. Tashi curled against her chest, pressing his face into her fur, waiting for the rise and fall he had known all his life.

It never came.

The sound he made then was thin and broken, a child's cry in a world that had stopped caring about children.

Chester arrived moments later, eyes wide, mouth drawn into something that looked like sorrow if you didn't look too closely.

"Oh," he murmured. "The poor thing."

He stepped closer, lowering his head, voice smooth as silk. "You must be terrified, little one. All alone now."

Tashi flinched but did not move.

"You can stay with me," Chester continued. "I'll protect you. I'll make sure nothing ever hurts you again."

Mama Bear's shadow fell across them both.

She did not bare her teeth. She did not roar. She simply stepped between Chester and the red panda, her massive body an immovable truth. Mowgli's blood drying on her fur.

"No," she said.

Chester blinked, surprised.

"I was only offering help."

"I know," Mama replied evenly.

She lowered herself beside Tashi, careful and slow, her great paw resting lightly over his shaking back. He turned into her without hesitation, clinging to her fur as though he had been waiting for her all along.

Mama's eyes lifted briefly—to the place where the red panda lay, to the direction of the gate, to the shadows where truths liked to hide.

Red pandas had not been on patrol. They had not been fighting. Something else had happened here.

Mama felt it settle into her bones, heavy and cold. She did not speak it. Not yet. Instead, she bent her head to Tashi's and hummed—a low, steady sound that had once soothed a frightened cub.

"You're safe," she murmured. "I've got you."

Behind her, Chester's smile thinned. And the fire crackled, waiting.

The fire had been rebuilt higher this time.

Not just for warmth—but for witnessing.

The fallen were laid in a wide arc before it: Aslan first, mane darkened by ash; Ernie beside him, massive even in death; Mowgli smaller than either, his youth making the space around him feel unbearably large. Others followed—names spoken softly, some never spoken at all.

The zoo gathered.

No councils. No arguments. Just bodies pressed close together, as if proximity alone might keep them from losing anyone else.

Chester stepped forward. He waited until every eye was on him. Until the silence grew uncomfortable. Then he bowed his head.

"Today," he began, voice low and steady, "we mourn giants."

He lifted his gaze, letting it sweep across the crowd. "Aslan, who led when fear would have scattered us. Ernie, who stood when standing meant certain death. And young Mowgli—" His voice softened, practiced but effective. "—who proved that courage is not measured in years, but in what you are willing to give."

Mama's breath hitched.

Chester continued. "They did not hesitate. They did not hide. They understood something essential."

He turned, slowly, deliberately, and gestured toward the far edge of the gathering.

"To her."

All eyes followed his paw.

The body of the red panda lay wrapped in leaves and cloth, small and easily overlooked among larger dead. Tashi stirred at Mama's side, confused, ears flattening.

"She was not a soldier," Chester said. "She was not on patrol. And yet—when the moment came—she was there."

Mama stiffened.

"She did not run," Chester went on. "She did not think, *this is not my duty.* She understood that the zoo does not survive because a few are brave—but because *all* are."

A murmur rippled through the animals.

"This," Chester said, lifting his voice, "is what unity looks like. No lines between fighters and non-fighters. No illusions that some are exempt from sacrifice."

Mama's jaw tightened. She said nothing.

"We cannot afford hesitation anymore," Chester declared. "The world beyond our gates has ended. The zoo is all that remains. And survival will demand more from us than comfort."

He turned back to the fire, raising his chin.

"Aslan is gone," he said solemnly. "Ernie is gone. Those who once led us into battle... are gone."

The pause was deliberate.

"But the zoo still stands."

He faced them again.

"And someone must stand *for it*."

No one cheered. No one objected either. Chester let the silence work for him.

"I will not pretend to replace them," he said, magnanimous. "But I will do what must be done to ensure their sacrifices were not in vain. I will protect this zoo. I will make the hard choices. I will carry the burden—so that none of you have to stand alone again."

The animals shifted, uneasy. Some looked to Mama. Some to Rocket. Some to Nej.

Then the ground trembled—not with fear, but with weight.

Happy stepped forward. The elephant's massive form cast a long shadow over the fire. His eyes were tired. Red-rimmed. He had lost friends too. Maybe more than anyone. He lowered his head slightly, a sign of respect—not submission.

"Chester is right about one thing," Happy said, voice deep and careful. "If we fracture now, we die."

A hush fell.

"We are scared," Happy continued. "We are angry. And we are grieving." His trunk curled inward briefly. "But grief can tear a herd apart if no one holds it together." He looked out over the zoo—not at Chester, but at everyone else.

"We need unity," he said. "Not tomorrow. Now."

A beat.

"And until we are strong enough to question leadership without tearing ourselves apart..." He paused, visibly pained. "We follow one voice."

Happy turned—slowly—and placed himself beside Chester.

"I stand with him," he said.

The effect was immediate. Whispers turned into nods. Nods into reluctant acceptance. Not belief—but relief. The relief of having *someone* to point to in the chaos.

Chester inclined his head humbly.

Mama did not move.

She stared at the fire. At her son. At the red panda who should never have been there. She felt the lie settling into the bones of the zoo—warm on the surface, poisonous underneath.

But today was not the day to speak it. Today, the zoo needed to stay together.

So Mama wrapped her paw tighter around Tashi.

And Chester smiled at the crowd he had just inherited.

Rebuilding

The days began to stack again.

Not as dates—none of them cared about calendars now—but as rhythms: sunrise, watering, patrol, fire, sleep. The zoo stopped feeling like a battlefield and started feeling like a place that *functioned*, even with the scars still fresh in the concrete and the missing shapes in the crowd.

Chester made sure everyone saw him when it mattered.

He would appear at the gates at dawn, pacing along the platforms with his chin lifted like the iron bars had been built for his reflection. He spoke often—about unity, about vigilance, about the weight of leadership. He insisted on standing where the work was most visible.

But it was the elephants who made the zoo run.

Happy's herd moved like living machinery. They heaved concrete barriers back into place with their trunks, nudged fallen steel into alignment, and pressed their weight into weak seams until the metal stopped groaning. Where claw and tooth had failed, mass and patience did not.

When the gates needed to be hauled upright again, it was elephants that did it. When the barricades needed to be repositioned to narrow the funnel, it was elephants that did it.

When the infected tested the perimeter with their dead hands, it was elephants that met them—lifting by ankles, swinging bodies like clubs, and tossing the ruined remains into the waiting pits without ever needing to step close enough to be bitten.

The patrols became an elephant business too. Not because the others were unwilling—but because everyone had seen what close combat cost. Big cats and apes had once been the first line.

Now they were names on ash.

So the elephants walked the wall, two at a time, their footfalls steady, their ears scanning the wind. Their eyes watched the dark places. Their trunks tested every chain, every knot, every hinge as they passed. They didn't roar. They didn't posture.

They just *held* the zoo together.

At the center of it all, AB never stopped moving.

Attenborough the beaver had dirt perpetually stuck to his whiskers and a permanent look of offended disappointment, as if reality itself was failing to meet his standards.

He inspected the gate every morning. Then again at noon. Then again at dusk. He checked the counterweights. He checked the pulley rope. He checked the reinforced weld points the elephants had bent back into place with brute force that made his careful calculations feel personally insulted.

"If any of you giants touch my mechanism again," AB muttered one afternoon, eyeing a slightly dented metal plate, "I will have you all reassigned to... to... tree moving. Permanently."

Happy rumbled something that might have been amusement and might have been exhaustion. He lifted the counterweight with delicate precision—delicate for an elephant, anyway—then set it down exactly where AB wanted it.

AB blinked, recalculated his worldview, and wrote something down in the dirt with a stick.

The scouts returned before sunset.

Tucker arrived first, slipping through the narrow section of gate with a proud, theatrical stride, as if he'd been invited to a press conference rather than sneaking past the dead.

Ira followed behind him, quieter, paws stained with mud, eyes bright with the sort of curiosity that kept him alive in a world that should've killed him years ago.

They stopped at the base of the platform where AB was already waiting, clipboard replaced by a slab of bark scratched with symbols only he cared about.

"Well?" AB demanded.

Tucker's ears perked up. He cleared his throat—unnecessarily dramatic—and announced, "We have good news and terrible news."

Ira snorted. "We have medium news."

Tucker ignored him. "The terrible news is that the dead are gathering north of the service road. A lot of them. Like... *end-of-the-world* a lot of them."

AB's eyes narrowed. "Numbers."

Tucker didn't waiver. "A... concerning amount."

Ira stepped forward. "Two herds. One about thirty, another about forty-five. They're not coordinated, but they're drifting toward the zoo because something out there is funneling them—noise, maybe, or movement. Could be a collapse somewhere that pushed them this direction."

AB's whiskers twitched. He looked from Ira to Tucker. "Routes?"

Ira pointed with one paw, drawing lines in the dirt. "This one circles by the river path. This one cuts behind the old maintenance buildings. They won't hit the main gate first. They'll test the west wall."

AB's head snapped toward the west.

Tucker leaned in, voice lowering like he was sharing a scandal. "And if they test the west wall, that means—"

"It means," AB interrupted, already moving, "we reinforce the west wall."

He scurried off with purpose, barking over his shoulder, "Tell the elephants. *Now.*"

Happy was already on his way.

Chester watched from the platform above, tail flicking lazily, eyes half-lidded like a king overseeing loyal subjects. When Happy passed below, Chester called down in a voice meant for the whole zoo to hear:

"Excellent work. Keep it up. The zoo is thriving under our leadership."

Happy didn't look up. He didn't have time for speeches. He had walls to hold.

Part 3: Visitor

The Girl at the Wall

Happy had just set the last slab into place when the sound reached him.

Not a moan. Not the wet, aimless growl of the dead. This sound was sharp. High. Frantic.

"Help! Please—help me!"

Happy froze, trunk lifting, ears flaring wide as the wind carried the sound again—closer this time. A human voice. He turned toward the tree line just as a small figure burst from the undergrowth. She was young, couldn't have seen more than eight summers.

Her shoes were wrong—one untied, one gone entirely. Her hair streamed behind her in a wild dark ribbon, her chest hitching as she ran with everything she had left. She stumbled, caught herself, and kept going, eyes locked on the thin curl of smoke rising above the zoo.

Behind her, the dead emerged. Five of them. Maybe six. Not fast—but relentless. Their bodies lurched through the trees, snagging on roots and branches, drawn forward by noise and movement and breath.

The girl screamed again and veered toward the wall, following it as though instinct knew what reason could not.

Happy didn't wait. He raised his trunk and let out a blast so loud it shook dust from the stonework—a warning call that rolled across the zoo like thunder.

Nej was in the air almost instantly. He tracked her, keeping pace as she ran around the perimeter, screaming for help.

"Shh. The more noise you make, the more you will attract. Keep going to the gate," Nej ordered the young girl.

The girl was too distracted with her own survival to even question that a bird was talking to her. She did as he said.

Chester arrived seconds later, slipping onto the platform with practiced ease, eyes already narrowing as he took in the scene.

"The wall," Chester said coolly. "Keep her outside."

Happy ignored him.

The girl reached the bend where the wall curved toward the gate. She slipped, fell to her knees, and turned—hands raised uselessly as the first zombie reached for her.

Happy moved.

He crossed the distance in long, ground-shaking strides. His trunk snapped out, coiling around the ankles of the nearest corpse. He swung it once—hard—and released. The body struck a tree with a sound like wet wood splitting.

Another zombie lunged.

Happy stepped forward and brought his trunk down with amazing velocity, crushing skull and spine in one decisive motion.

Two more staggered closer.

He grabbed one and used it as a weapon, smashing it into the other until neither moved again.

The last one tried to crawl.

Happy lifted it and hurled it into the pit beyond the wall.

Silence fell, broken only by the girl's ragged breathing.

She stared up at the elephant, eyes wide, fear flickering into something else—wonder, maybe. Relief.

Nej swooped down, landing on the wall near her.

"Are you hurt?" Nej asked gently.

The girl shook her head hard. "No. No, I—I don't think so."

"Show me," Nej said.

She held out her arms. Turned. Lifted her hair. Pulled at her torn shirt with shaking fingers. No blood. No bites.

"My mom and dad were with me," she said quickly, words tumbling over each other. "We were hiding, but then they came out of nowhere and—" Her voice cracked. "We got separated. I ran. I just kept running."

Chester leaned forward. "That's unfortunate," he said. "But humans bring danger. We cannot risk opening the gate."

The girl looked at him then—really looked—and something about his chuff made her question her safety.

Happy didn't. He lowered his trunk gently, curling it around her middle like a seatbelt. The girl yelped in surprise—and then laughed. A real laugh. Bright and unafraid.

She clutched the elephant's trunk as Happy lifted her high, higher than she had ever been, and stepped over the gate with careful precision.

Nej followed, wings beating fast.

Chester's tail lashed once.

The Council Gathers

They met near the fire, as they always did now. Not in a circle—never quite that organized—but close enough that no one stood alone.

The girl sat near Happy's foreleg, legs tucked under her, hands wrapped around a warm cup of water someone had found for her. She watched everything with wide, curious eyes, fear slowly giving way to fascination.

Mama sat nearby, one paw resting protectively behind the girl.

Nej perched above, quiet and observant.

AB stood apart, already irritated.

"This is reckless," Chester said, pacing just enough to be noticed. "We agreed the zoo is safer without humans."

"We agreed the zoo is safer without *carelessness*," Rocket replied flatly.

"She will draw more of them," Chester insisted. "Noise. Movement. Emotion. Humans always do."

Happy spoke without raising his voice. "She was being hunted."

"That is not our responsibility."

Mama's head lifted. "It became our responsibility when she reached the wall. She asked for help. She needs us."

Some animals murmured agreement. Others shifted uneasily.

A zebra snorted.

The girl shrank slightly. Although she couldn't understand what was being said, it was clear enough to her that they *were* talking and about *her*.

Nej tilted his head. "What is your name?" he asked her softly.

"Eliza," she said. "Eliza Maren Jones-Walker."

The name meant nothing to most of them. But Nej went very still. Chester noticed. His eyes narrowed.

"We are not equipped to care for her," Chester said smoothly. "She is small. Fragile. A liability."

AB cleared his throat—sharp, annoyed. "That's incorrect."

Every head turned.

"I have been recalculating the west wall," AB continued, already irritated that he had to explain something obvious. "There are stress points we cannot reach. Valves we cannot adjust. Mechanisms that require hands, not hooves or trunks."

He glanced at Eliza. "She has hands."

Chester scoffed. "You're suggesting we keep a human child because you need a tool?"

"I'm suggesting," AB snapped, "that she is uniquely suited to tasks none of you can perform. And that ignoring useful data because of fear is inefficient."

Happy rumbled softly. Approval.

Rocket nodded once. "Efficiency keeps us alive."

Mama looked down at Eliza, who was staring at the fire, mesmerized.

"She can stay," Mama said. "For now."

The room stilled.

Chester opened his mouth— but before he could say anything, Mama added, "And we will watch, all of us."

The decision settled, not unanimously—but firmly enough.

Eliza looked up, eyes shining. "I can help," she said quickly. "I promise. I'm really good at fixing things."

Happy lowered his trunk toward her, and she leaned against it instinctively.

Chester forced a smile.

"Of course," he mumbled. "Welcome... temporarily."

Nej watched him closely.

The fire crackled. And the zoo, once more, changed course.

Eliza

A week passed—not marked by dates, but by habits returning.

The west wall became Eliza's place.

Every morning, she followed Happy to the wall. She carried tools that were almost too heavy for her and handed them up anyway, stubborn in the way only children could be. She learned where to stand without being told, learned when to move back just by the way the elephants shifted their weight.

Nej was almost always nearby. "Hold still," he would say from the wall, watching the animals work. "Happy says the plate will slide."

Eliza nodded and stepped aside before the slab moved, not because she understood the words exactly, but because Happy's trunk had gone rigid and his ears had angled forward—a warning she'd learned to read faster than language.

When Nej wasn't there, Eliza still managed.

She couldn't hear instructions, but she watched tails, ears, shoulders. She learned that a tiger's stillness meant something very different from a bear's. She learned that when Rocket went quiet and withdrew into his shell just a fraction, it meant stop—slow down—think.

Sometimes she spoke anyway. "It's okay," she'd murmur while tightening a bolt or brushing dust from a crack. "I've got it. I won't mess it up."

The animals didn't answer. But they stayed. And that felt like an answer.

Tashi followed her everywhere.

At first, he watched from a distance—curled up beneath Mama's watchful gaze, eyes tracking Eliza as she moved. When she laughed, his ears twitched. When she tripped and caught herself, his tail flicked.

One afternoon, she sat down near the panda enclosure with a piece of chalk she'd found and began drawing on a flat stone—circles, badly shaped animals, a gate that was far too tall and crooked.

Tashi crept closer.

She noticed him without startling, the way kids sometimes do when they recognize another kid. She slid the chalk toward him.

"Wanna draw?"

He didn't understand the words. But he understood the invitation.

He picked up the chalk with careful paws and scratched a clumsy spiral into the stone. It wasn't much—but when Eliza gasped like it was the most amazing thing she'd ever seen, Tashi chirred in delight.

They spent the afternoon like that—drawing, erasing, starting over. Sometimes they just sat shoulder to shoulder, watching shadows move across the ground.

Two small bodies in a world built for bigger, crueler things.

Mama watched from a distance, chest tight, something like relief settling where grief had lived.

Eliza changed the zoo in quiet ways.

Animals lingered longer near the fire when she was there. The smaller ones stopped scattering at sudden movement. Even the tigers—aloof as ever—watched her with something like curiosity rather than calculation.

She waved at everyone. Not because she expected a response—but because it felt wrong not to.

When she laughed, it wasn't careful. It wasn't quiet. It rang out in bright, reckless bursts that reminded the zoo of something it had almost forgotten: that joy could exist without permission.

Nej noticed first.

"She hums when she works," he told Rocket one evening.

Rocket grunted. "Annoying."

"But steady," Nej added.

Rocket paused. "Yes," he admitted. "Steady."

Happy liked her because she talked to him even when Nej wasn't translating—telling him about clouds that looked like animals, about how high she felt riding his trunk that first day, about how the zoo smelled different in the mornings.

Happy didn't understand the words. But he understood the tone. And that was enough.

By the end of the week, the west wall stood stronger than it had ever been.

AB inspected it twice a day and found fewer reasons to complain. Tucker still returned with alarming reports. Ira still returned with accurate ones. Chester still made appearances and speeches.

But the zoo no longer felt like it was holding its breath.

Eliza sat on the wall one evening, legs swinging, Tashi pressed against her side, Nej perched above them both.

"I think it's working," she said softly, watching the sun dip low. "All of it."

Nej tilted his head, listening to sounds only he could translate.

"Maybe," he said. "For now."

Eliza smiled anyway. Because for kids like her—and like Tashi—*for now* was everything.

One of Us

The trouble started small. It usually did.

Eliza was carrying a coil of wire toward the west wall when she heard the hiss—sharp, defensive, unnecessary. A young porcupine had wandered too close to the work area, bristling at nothing in particular, frozen in the open where it absolutely did not belong.

The wall loomed above them. Happy was adjusting a slab overhead. AB was halfway inside a maintenance gap, muttering to himself. No one else had noticed yet.

Eliza did.

She saw the way the porcupine's quills flared—not in fear, but confusion. She saw how close it was to the drop where stones sometimes shifted loose. She saw the danger not because it was loud or dramatic, but because it was *avoidable*.

Eliza remembered the tree first.

It had been old—older than the park itself, her father once said—with bark so thick and folded it looked like it had grown muscles. Its roots pushed up through the grass in long, knotted veins, perfect for lining up her stuffed animals like an audience. A bear. A rabbit with one bent ear. A faded elephant whose tag had been worn smooth by her fingers.

She sat cross-legged at the base of the trunk, humming to herself, moving the toys in careful, serious patterns. The world was warm. Sunlight sifted down through the leaves in soft, flickering pieces. Somewhere nearby, her mother sat on a bench, legs crossed, phone forgotten in her lap as she watched.

Above her, laughter.

Two older boys were climbing the tree, their sneakers scraping against bark, their voices loud and fearless. Eliza glanced up once, squinting, then went back to her game. The tree felt big enough for all of them. Trees always did.

Then came the sound.

A sharp crack—dry and sudden—like a giant snapping its fingers.

Eliza looked up.

Her mother was already running.

She didn't remember her mother standing or shouting her name. Only the way her face changed as she crossed the grass, fear cutting through it so fast it felt like it tore the air open.

One of the boys jumped.

He dropped from a branch just above Eliza, landing hard but safe against the trunk. The bark shuddered. Leaves shook loose and spun down around them.

Another crack—louder this time.

The branch groaned, a deep, breaking sound that seemed to come from inside the tree itself.

Eliza froze.

She didn't know how to move fast yet. Didn't know which way was away.

Her mother reached her in two strides.

Then there was only weight and arms and the smell of her mother's shampoo as she was pressed tight against her chest. Too tight. So tight it hurt.

The branch fell.

It crashed into the ground with a sound Eliza would remember forever—wood splitting, dirt exploding, something solid meeting something fragile.

Her mother screamed.

Later—much later—there were sirens. Red and white lights washing over the park. Voices talking too quickly. A blanket that wasn't theirs wrapped around both of them. Eliza remembered staring at her stuffed elephant lying in the grass, half-buried in leaves, while strangers lifted her mother onto a stretcher.

Then the memory shifted.

Hospitals always smelled the same. Clean and sharp and wrong.

Eliza's feet didn't touch the floor as she sat in the chair beside the bed. Her legs swung slowly, back and forth, back and forth. Her mother lay still beneath white sheets, one arm wrapped in thick bandages. Machines hummed softly, like they were whispering to themselves.

Her dad sat close, one hand resting on the edge of the mattress, the other steady on Eliza's knee.

"Daddy?" she asked.

"Yes, sweetheart."

"Why did Mommy do that?"

He looked at her. "Do what?"

"Cover me," Eliza said. "She got hurt."

Her father was quiet for a moment. Eliza watched his face while he thought, the way his eyes went somewhere far away before coming back.

"Because she's your mother," he said finally. "And that means it's her responsibility to protect you."

Eliza frowned. "Even if it hurts?"

"Yes," he said. "Especially then."

The bed shifted.

Eliza gasped as her mother stirred, eyelids fluttering open. Her face was pale, but when she saw Eliza, her mouth curved into a tired smile.

"Hey," her mother whispered.

Eliza slid forward in the chair, clutching the blanket. "Mommy?"

"I'm here," her mother said, voice rough but warm. "I heard you talking."

Eliza looked between her parents. "Daddy said it's your job to protect me."

Her mother nodded slowly. "That's right."

"But you got hurt," Eliza said, her voice very small now.

Her mother reached out with her uninjured hand, fingers brushing Eliza's cheek. They were warm. Still real.

"There is nothing," her mother said softly, "nothing at all, that I wouldn't do to keep you safe."

Eliza leaned into her touch, pressing her face into her mother's palm as if memorizing it.

Years later, when the memory came back to her in flashes—wood breaking, arms closing, pain shouted into the air—this was the part she held onto.

Not the scream.

Not the sirens.

Just the certainty in her mother's voice, steady as the tree had once been.

"Eliza—wait—"

Nej's warning came too late.

Eliza dropped the wire and ran.

She slid between the porcupine and the wall, arms wide, back to the stone, shielding it with her own body. Gravel skittered down past her shoulder. A loose chunk of concrete fell—missing her head by inches.

The porcupine squeaked and tried to turn.

"It's okay," Eliza whispered, hands shaking but steady. "You're okay. I've got you."

Happy froze mid-adjustment, every muscle locked.

AB swore—loudly.

The porcupine scuttled away at last, disappearing into the brush exactly as it would have done without help.

A still quiet followed.

Eliza stayed where she was, pressed to the wall, breathing hard, heart hammering so loud she was sure everyone could hear it.

Nej landed in front of her.

"Why did you do that?" he asked—not angry, not scolding. Just trying to understand.

She looked up at him, dust streaked across her cheek, eyes bright with leftover fear and something fiercer underneath.

"My dad used to say something," she said quietly. "Whenever I asked why he always helped people who didn't ask for it."

Nej tilted his head.

"He said, *we protect those who depend on us.*"

The words settled into the air.

"I know I can't lift walls or fight monsters," Eliza continued. "But... we're a family. Families don't wait to see if someone needs help before they care. We just do."

She glanced around, suddenly self-conscious. "And if we all depend on each other... then that counts. Right?"

No one moved.

Then Mama stepped forward.

She lowered her massive head until she was level with Eliza's eyes. Her breath was warm, steady. Approval lived there—not loud, not dramatic. Certain.

Happy rumbled low in his chest.

Nej swallowed.

That night, they gathered where the fire had once burned hottest. The place where ash still marked the stone.

Nej guided Eliza to the center, his wing brushing her shoulder gently, the way he did when he wanted her to pay attention.

The animals formed a loose ring around her.

No speeches. No commands.

Mama stepped forward and pressed her paw into the ash. Slowly, deliberately, she traced letters—not perfect, not clean. But unmistakable.

WE PROTECT THOSE WHO DEPEND ON US

Eliza's breath caught.

Nej leaned close. "She taught us that before she died," he said softly. "For us."

The animals lowered their heads.

Happy dipped his trunk.

Rocket touched the ash with one claw.

Each of them acknowledged the words in their own way—some bowing, some touching the ground, some simply standing still.

Mama stepped aside.

Nej gestured for Eliza.

With shaking hands, Eliza knelt and pressed her palm into the ash beside the words. It coated her skin, dark and warm, clinging like memory.

"You are one of us," Nej said.

The zoo answered—not with noise, but presence.

For the first time since the world fell apart, everything felt *right*.

Morning came gently. Birds stirred. Light crept over stone and fur and ash-marked ground.

Eliza was helping Tashi stack smooth rocks near the path when the sound carried over the wall.

"Eliza!" A man's voice. Hoarse. Urgent.

"Eliza! Sweetheart!" Another voice joined it—a woman this time, raw with hope and terror braided together.

The zoo froze. Eliza's hands went still. Outside the wall, the voices called her name again.

And the day changed.

Reunion

Eliza reached the gate before anyone could stop her.

"Dad!" she shouted, already running.

Happy shifted instinctively, careful not to block her, and the elephants parted just enough for her to see them—two figures standing beyond the wall, thinner than they should have been, clothes torn and dust-streaked, eyes wild with disbelief and hope.

"Eliza—oh my God—Eliza!"

Her mother dropped to her knees the moment she saw her, hands shaking, tears cutting clean lines through the grime on her face. Eliza hit her at full speed, arms wrapping tight, the impact knocking the breath out of both of them.

Her father folded over them, one hand pressed to the back of Eliza's head as if afraid she might vanish again.

"We thought—" her mother sobbed. "We thought—"

"I'm okay," Eliza said quickly, pulling back just enough to look at them. "I really am. I helped fix the wall. And I met so many animals. And they're really smart, and kind, and—" She gestured wildly behind her. "They're my family."

Her parents followed her gaze.

The zoo watched them in return.

Happy stood like a living pillar near the gate. Mama's eyes never left Eliza. Rocket sat half in shadow. Tigers lingered at the edges, unreadable.

Nej landed on the gatepost.

"Eliza," he said gently, "the council must meet."

Her smile faltered—but only slightly.

"Oh. Right," she said, nodding. Then she turned back to her parents, hopeful again. "That's okay. They'll understand. You can stay. We can all stay."

Nej did not answer that.

They gathered where the ash still marked the stone.

Eliza sat between her parents, holding both their hands. She couldn't understand the animals' words, but she felt the way the space tightened, the way old wounds stirred beneath the calm.

Nej stood where all could see him. The animals who spoke in favor went first. Mama stepped forward, her presence heavy and undeniable. Nej translated.

"She says the cub has proven herself. She risked herself for others. She brought light back to the zoo."

Happy followed, voice low and steady. "Eliza made the work lighter. The walls stronger. The days better."

Rocket spoke next, gruff but sincere. "She listens. That she watches before acting. That is rare."

Even Tucker contributed, animated and intense. Nej relayed it with effort.

"He says morale matters. He says fear feeds the dead as much as noise does."

Ira spoke after—short, precise. "Eliza improves efficiency. Fewer mistakes. Fewer panics."

Eliza squeezed her parents' hands, heart pounding.

Then Chester stepped forward. The air changed. Nej's feathers smoothed as he listened.

"Humans bring chaos. Their presence draws the dead. That history proves this." Chester paced as he spoke, tail flicking, voice smooth and persuasive.

"He says one good human does not erase generations of cages, chains, and cruelty. That sentiment is dangerous," Nej translated.

Murmurs rippled through the zoo.

Eliza's father stood. "May I speak?" he asked softly.

Nej tilted his head, listening, then nodded. "You may."

The man stepped forward alone.

"I won't pretend I deserve your trust," he began. "But some of you may remember me. I was a doctor here. I trained Nadege. I worked beside her for decades. My name is Dr. Daniel Jones-Walker."

At his name, several animals stirred.

"This place used to be like home. Nadege and I bonded over our shared compassion for all of you. *Nou pwoteje sa ki depann de nou.*"

The man swallowed.

"But I also know humans can be cruel. My family has a history with animals," he said carefully. "More than a hundred years ago, my great-grandfather was chased from his farm."

Some of the animals leaned forward.

"Not because he was kind," Daniel said. "But because he wasn't."

A hush fell.

"He was cruel. He believed animals existed only to serve. He paid for that belief—and so did they." Daniel clasped his hands behind his back. "My family has spent every generation since trying to learn from that failure. To undo it. To be better than the lesson he left us."

He looked around the circle.

"I don't ask you to forget that history. I ask you to honor it—by choosing what kind of future you want." He bowed his head. "If you say we must leave, we will. We will respect your decision."

No one spoke.

Chester stepped forward again, seizing the moment. Nej translated, slower now.

"Chester says the man's story proves the point. That even good intentions lead to suffering. That mercy now will invite ruin later."

The balance tipped. Mama did not step forward again. Neither did Happy. The decision settled—not loudly, but finally.

Nej turned to Eliza.

"They say your parents cannot stay," he told her gently.

Her breath caught. She nodded anyway.

Eliza moved through the zoo slowly.

She hugged Happy's trunk, pressing her face into the warm, steady curve of it. She scratched Rocket's shell just the way he liked. She sat with Mama, forehead against fur, neither of them needing words.

Tashi followed her everywhere.

When she knelt in front of him, he chirred softly, confused and hurting. "I'll remember you," she whispered, touching her forehead to his. "Always."

Nej landed on her shoulder last.

"You belong here," he said quietly.

"I know," she replied.

She took one last look at the wall, the fire pit, the ash-marked ground where her handprint still lingered. Then she took her parents' hands. The gate opened, and the family stepped through.

Behind them, the zoo closed again—quiet, watchful, changed forever.

Surviving

The zoo settled again. It always did.

But this time, the settling felt heavier—like dust after a collapse, when the structure still stands but the air never quite clears. The routines returned, but they moved through them without the lightness Eliza had carried so effortlessly. Work was done. Patrols walked. Fires burned.

Everything functioned, but everything felt grayer, duller.

The infirmary stayed quiet.

Rocket moved with the same slow precision as always, but he lingered longer by Jwaye's side now. The orangutan lay propped against woven bedding, bandages clean, wounds no longer angry with infection. His breathing was steadier. His fever had broken days ago.

Physically, he was improving. Spiritually, he was hollow.

Jwaye stared at the ceiling more often than not, eyes unfocused, hands resting open as if waiting for something to fall into them. He ate when prompted.

Drank when reminded. Lived because his body insisted on it—not because he did.

Rocket adjusted a dressing and paused. "You are winning," he said quietly.

Jwaye did not answer.

"You survived," Rocket continued. "Many did not."

Still nothing.

Rocket sighed, ancient and tired. "Survival is not the same as wanting to stay."

Jwaye's fingers twitched at that.

"Mowgli wanted you here," Rocket added—not as comfort, but as fact.

Jwaye turned his face away, a low, broken sound catching in his chest.

Rocket left him then—not because he didn't care, but because sometimes care meant allowing grief to breathe.

At the west wall, problems accumulated. AB stood on his hind legs, tapping a section of stone with a stick, scowling.

"This is not catastrophic," he announced. "But it is *concerning*."

Happy loomed beside him, trunk tracing the seam Eliza used to check every morning.

"It is slipping," Happy rumbled. "Only a little. But little becomes more."

AB flicked his tail irritably. "She noticed things before instruments did."

Happy said nothing. They both knew why.

Without Eliza's small hands tightening bolts, clearing grit, brushing debris from cracks, the wall had begun to do what all unattended things eventually did—wear down.

"We can compensate," AB muttered. "But it will take longer. And longer is dangerous."

Happy looked toward the tree line beyond the wall. "That brings us to timing," he said.

Tucker and Ira arrived just before dusk.

Tucker was animated, tail snapping, ears high with urgency. Ira followed at his usual measured pace, mud still clinging to his paws.

Nej landed nearby, listening.

Tucker spoke first—fast, sharp, insistent. "The herds are closer. Bigger. Moving with purpose."

Ira spoke next, voice low and steady. "Two herds have merged. Sixty to seventy now. No deviation in path."

AB stiffened. "Timeframe?"

Ira answered without embellishment. "Within a week." The word settled like ash.

Happy closed his eyes for a moment, then opened them again.

"We will hold," he said—not bravely, not foolishly. Just stating a responsibility.

Nej looked toward the infirmary, where Jwaye lay staring at shadows. Rocket felt the shift in the air and said nothing. The zoo would adjust. It always did. But as night fell, the fire burned lower than it used to—and no one laughed at the sparks.

Stone Remembers

The council space was quieter than usual. Not solemn—*tense.*

Happy stood closest to the map scratched into the dirt, trunk hovering just above the markings AB had added just before. Nej perched on a beam overhead, feathers sleek, eyes sharp. Mama sat opposite Chester, her bulk grounded, unmoving.

Chester lounged near the fire as if it were a throne, tail flicking lazily.

Nej spoke first.

"The west herds are moving again," he said, voice clear. "Faster than before."

AB snapped his teeth in irritation and pointed to the map with a stick. "Two confirmed clusters," Nej continued, translating. "One has merged with strays. Numbers are growing, not shrinking."

Happy shifted his weight, the ground murmuring beneath him. "They're not wandering," he added. "They're *pressing.*"

Chester barely looked up.

"We reinforced the wall," he said smoothly. "Multiple times. The elephants have done excellent work." He nodded toward Happy, magnanimous. "What more do you want?"

AB chittered sharply, scribbling new marks into the dirt.

Nej frowned. "AB says the wall is strong—but not infinite. Pressure compounds. Fatigue sets in. Stone remembers stress."

"Everything remembers stress," Chester replied. "That's life."

Mama's head lifted. Her voice was low. Controlled. "This isn't philosophy. This is warning."

Chester finally looked at her, a thin smile forming. "Aww. You worry too much."

Happy's trunk curled inward. "If the west wall fails—"

"It won't," Chester interrupted.

Nej's feathers ruffled. "You don't *know* that."

Chester rose slowly, stretching as though inconvenienced. "I *know* we've done everything reasonable. We cannot panic every time the dead shuffle in our direction."

Mama stood then, towering. "You dismissed the gate. You dismissed patrol spacing. You dismissed

Aslan's caution." Her eyes burned. "And every time, someone paid the price."

The fire popped.

For a moment—just a moment—Chester's mask slipped.

Then it returned, flawless.

"We cannot live in fear," he said calmly. "Leadership means knowing when to stop reacting." He smiled around the circle. "The zoo is stable. The wall is stable. This conversation is over."

Silence followed—not agreement, but resignation. Happy lowered his trunk. AB stopped writing. Nej looked away.

Mama held Chester's gaze for a long second longer than necessary—then turned aside.

There was nothing else to do. And Chester knew it.

The climb was effortless.

Chester moved across Tiger Mountain like it had been built for him—stone ledges catching his weight perfectly, every path familiar, every height offering exactly what he wanted: distance.

Perspective. From the summit, the zoo spread below him like a model. Walls. Fires. Movement. Order.

Beyond it— Chaos.

Roving herds dragged themselves through the outer roads, shapes clustering and separating like stains in water. Chester watched them with clinical interest, not fear.

"Too many," he murmured sarcastically. "Too stupid. Too slow." He paced the ridge, tail high, eyes never stopping.

If the wall fell, it wouldn't be sudden. There would be sound. Confusion. Panic. The elephants would rush. The others would hesitate.

And Chester?

Chester would already be moving.

He traced the escape routes in his mind—the gaps, the climbable sections, the blind spots the beavers never quite accounted for. The places where strength mattered less than *speed*.

The zoo below looked small from up here. Fragile. Replaceable.

"I gave them leadership," he said softly, admiring the way his voice echoed back to him. "That's more than they deserved."

He sat, tail curling neatly around his paws, watching the dead drift closer.

If the wall held, he would rule. If it didn't— Well. Kings survived.

Everyone else was optional.

Part 4: The Reckoning

Breach

The west wall groaned but did not give.

Bodies pressed against it—too many, too relentless—but the stone held. Hope flickered. The animals surged there, striking, pushing, dragging hands and teeth away from the cracks. The wall shook, but it stood.

Then the sound changed. Not pressure. Movement.

Nej's cry cut through the air, sharp and panicked. The wave wasn't breaking anymore—it was flowing. They were going around. The front gate failed with a sound like the sky tearing.

Iron screamed as it ripped free from stone. The barricades buckled, then vanished beneath bodies. The funnel collapsed inward, swallowing itself as the herds surged through in a living avalanche of rot and hunger.

Chaos exploded.

Happy charged. He didn't pause for even a moment. He never did.

The elephant met the wave head-on, his tusks and trunk carving space where none should exist. He lifted bodies and hurled them aside. He crushed skulls beneath his feet. He roared—low, furious, unafraid.

But there were too many.

Hands latched onto his legs. Teeth scraped uselessly at hide. More climbed. More piled. The wave closed around him, swallowing gray skin and ivory until all that could be seen was movement.

Then nothing.

A terrible stillness rippled through the zoo. Happy was gone. For one heartbeat, the animals froze. Then something shifted. They didn't break.

They raged.

Enclosures were flung open—not in panic, but with intent. Gates became traps. Corridors became choke points. Animals lured the dead inside spaces meant to contain life and sealed them shut. Predators struck from above, below, from angles the living would never consider.

This wasn't fear anymore. This was resolve.

Mama Bear tore through the crowd, blood matted in her fur, her breath a thunderous snarl. She struck with prejudice, without mercy.

I won't lose anyone else.

Then—clarity. Her head snapped up.

"Tashi."

The world narrowed. She saw him—small, cornered, pressed back against fallen debris. A zombie lurched toward him, arms grasping, mouth opening.

For a split second, Mama Bear wasn't here. She was somewhere else. She saw her son. She saw Mowgli's last stand—alone, brave, trying to be bigger than he was.

The memory didn't weaken her. It forged her.

She charged.

Two leapt onto her back, claws raking, teeth snapping. She bucked and rolled, slamming one into the ground, crushing another beneath her weight.

But she was too far.

She wouldn't make it in time.

Then—a scream. Human. High. Desperate. Eliza's mother.

She came from above—leaping down into the space between Tashi and the zombie, knife already in motion. The zombie turned, faster than she expected.

It bit her. Deep. Blood poured down her neck, dark and immediate. She didn't scream again. She drove the knife upward, again and again, until the zombie collapsed with her. She fell to her knees. Then forward.

"Eliza," she breathed.

Eliza was already there—hands shaking, pressing uselessly against the wound.

"No," Eliza sobbed. "No, no, no—"

Tashi pressed close, small hands trembling but present. Together, they held her as her breath slowed, then stopped.

Silence—brief, terrible.

They looked up. They were surrounded.

Mama Bear roared.

The sound tore through the chaos—raw, furious, *grieving*. She threw herself into the middle of the herd, claws flashing, teeth tearing. They swarmed her, scratching, biting, dragging her down inch by inch.

She did not stop. When she finally staggered, it wasn't because she chose to.

A gunshot cracked the air. Then another.

Eliza's father—Daniel—burst through the crowd, firing with precision born of panic and love.

Together, he and Mama Bear cleared the remaining dead, bodies falling away until there was space again.

Mama Bear took one last step. And collapsed.

She was breathing. Barely.

Then the air shifted. A presence.

Chester.

The tiger emerged from the smoke and ruin, eyes bright, posture loose and confident. He circled slowly, placing himself between Eliza and escape.

Daniel raised the gun. "Easy," he said, voice shaking. "Easy."

Chester's lips pulled back in something that might have been a smile.

"You shouldn't have come back," Chester purred. "Now they'll look to you. And this—" he glanced around "—is my kingdom."

Daniel didn't understand the words. He understood the intent.

Tashi stepped forward, trembling but defiant. "Chester, please don't. They're family."

Chester flicked his gaze down.

"Then I'll kill you too," he said softly. "Just like I did Aslan. Just like I did your mother. Then you can be with your family."

The ground moved. A shadow loomed behind Chester. A mighty trumpet sounded, and Chester turned to see Happy standing as powerful and majestic as he ever had been.

He wrapped his trunk around Chester's hind legs and lifted.

Chester yowled, claws scrabbling at the air. He twisted and struck, raking Happy's trunk with a claw. Happy bellowed in pain and dropped the tiger.

Chester hit the ground hard, stunned.

He turned—

And the dart hit him in the neck. Chester froze. Then collapsed.

The infirmary smelled of ash, crushed leaves, and antiseptic pulled from a world that no longer existed.

Mama Bear lay on her side, massive chest rising and falling in shallow, uneven breaths. Her fur was matted dark where claws and teeth had torn through it. Rocket had done what he could—packed wounds with poultices, bound what could be bound—but even he had gone quiet now, standing watch with the solemn patience of something very old.

Jwaye stirred. Pain came first. Then memory. He lifted his head and saw her.

"Mama," he whispered.

One eye opened. Clouded, but still warm.

"There you are," Mama said softly. Her voice was rough, but steady. "I was worried I wouldn't get to see you awake again."

Jwaye struggled to sit, shame flooding his face. "I'm sorry," he said. "I should have—"

She lifted a paw just enough to stop him. "No," she said. "You stayed. You lived."

Her breath hitched, then settled. "I'm glad you're okay," she continued. "That matters more than you know."

Jwaye's eyes burned. "Mowgli—he ran so fast."

"I know," Mama said. "And I am proud of him. Proud beyond words."

She turned her head just slightly, as if looking at something far away.

"He saw you in danger, and he chose love over fear. That was his strength." Her gaze returned to Jwaye, sharp despite the pain. "And that strength is yours now."

Jwaye shook his head. "I don't deserve it."

Mama's paw pressed weakly against the floor.

"You don't get to decide that," she said. "Wasting the life he saved would dishonor his sacrifice. Living well honors it."

Jwaye broke then, pressing his forehead to the ground beside her.

"I won't waste it," he said through tears. "I promise."

Mama smiled. "That's all I needed to hear."

Jwaye stayed a moment longer, then rose. He bowed his head, touched her paw gently, and left the infirmary without looking back—carrying her words with him like something sacred.

The doorway darkened again. Small footsteps. Tashi stepped inside. He froze when he saw her. Mama's gaze softened instantly.

"There you are, little red one," she murmured.

Tashi rushed forward and pressed close, curling beside her chest like he had so many nights before. His voice shook.

"I was scared," he said. "But I didn't run."

"I saw," Mama said. "I saw you stand when it mattered."

She gathered what strength she had left and nudged him closer.

"I am proud of you," she said. "For standing up to Chester. For protecting your family. For being brave even when you were afraid."

Tashi's tears soaked into her fur.

"I didn't want to lose you too."

Mama exhaled, long and slow.

"You didn't," she said. "Not the part that matters." She rested her forehead against his.

"Remember this," she whispered. "Family isn't who came before you. It's who stands beside you."

Tashi nodded, unable to speak.

Mama's breathing slowed.

Then stilled.

Rocket lowered his head.

Outside, the fire crackled. The zoo went on.

But in the infirmary, a matriarch had finished her work—and left behind a family strong enough to carry it forward.

Justice

Chester woke to iron.

Cold bars pressed close on all sides, the cage barely large enough for him to sit without brushing metal. It smelled of antiseptic and old fear—something scavenged from the medical building, repurposed with intention. His tail flicked once, irritated more than afraid.

Around him, the council had gathered.

They stood in a loose circle, some wounded, some soot-stained, some still shaking from what they had survived. Firelight from the pits outside the gate flickered across fur and feathers, throwing long shadows that made the space feel smaller than it was.

The arguments had already begun.

"Kill him," Jwaye said, voice breaking through the low murmur like a snapped branch. The young orangutan stood rigid, hands clenched. "He doesn't get to walk away. He killed Aslan. He caused the breach. Mowgli died because of him. Everyone who fought—everyone who burned—burned because of him."

A low rumble of agreement moved through the group.

"He'll do it again," someone said.

"Or worse," another answered.

Chester rolled his eyes.

Then Eliza spoke.

Her voice was small, but it carried.

"If we kill him," she said, stepping forward, "then we become what we're afraid of. He's wrong. He's hurt people. But if we decide that anyone who hurts us deserves to die, then where does it stop?"

Chester turned his head slowly, annoyance flashing across his face. A *child* speaking. A human. He schooled his expression into something close to humility.

"She's right," he said smoothly. "I made mistakes. But we're all frightened. We're all trying to survive."

Inside, he smiled. *If this saves my life, I'll let the cub talk.*

The council considereded.

Finally, the decision settled—not cleanly, but firmly.

"You will be banished," came the judgment. "You will leave the zoo immediately. If you return, you will be executed."

Attenborough the beaver tilted his head and added dryly, "And do mind the pits outside the gate. We're burning the infected there. Very unpleasant way to go."

A few animals huffed despite themselves.

Chester's ears flattened.

The cage door creaked open.

That was when he lunged.

It was fast—pure instinct and rage, all pretense gone. Straight for Eliza.

The elephant's trunk lashed out and wrapped around Chester midair—one coil across his forelegs, tightening around his neck. Chester struck wildly, claws flashing, raking Happy's trunk hard enough to draw a sharp bellow of pain.

But Happy did not let go.

The zoo went silent.

Happy turned his head slightly toward Eliza.

"Sometimes," he said gently, "protecting those who depend on us means protecting them from those who are close to us."

He did not raise his voice. He did not look at Chester again. Happy walked.

Each step toward the burning pits was deliberate. Final. Chester thrashed and screamed as the heat grew unbearable, the firelight reflecting in his eyes as he finally understood.

Happy released him. The flames took the rest. No one spoke.

Eliza stood frozen, tears streaming down her face. This time, it was Daniel that translated for his daughter. Daniel stepped beside her and placed a hand on her shoulder, his voice barely audible.

"We protect those who depend on us."

The fire crackled. Behind them, the zoo stood—wounded, grieving, but intact.

And this time, the commandment held.

A New Dawn

The repairs took days. Not frantic days. Deliberate ones.

Daniel moved alongside the animals as if he had always belonged there—directing when needed, listening when he didn't understand, trusting the instincts of those who had survived when theory had failed. Beyond the broken gate, he and Happy hauled what the old world had abandoned: steel beams from fallen signs, rebar from cracked sidewalks, fencing torn loose from forgotten construction sites. Things meant to divide people were dragged back and made useful.

Happy learned quickly.

With Daniel guiding placement and the beavers calculating load, the elephant became precision itself—lifting, setting, bracing. The walls rose thicker than before, layered with stone and steel, designed not just to stop a charge but to *absorb* it. Where the gate had once been ornamental, it was now honest.

The zoo did not pretend it would never fall again. It built as though it intended to endure anyway. When the work was done, the fires were prepared.

Rocket oversaw the infirmary one last time, ensuring that every body—every claw, every feather, every scrap of fur—was treated with intention. He said little, but when he spoke, the younger animals listened. The world had ended once already, after all. He was proof that something could keep going afterward.

Jwaye stood tall now. Still gentle. Still grieving. But his eyes no longer searched the ground. He had taken on the care of the youngest injured, repeating Mama's lessons with a patience that surprised even him. When the fire was lit, he was the first to bow his head—not in despair, but in promise.

Nej circled overhead, then settled where all could see him.

He did not give a long speech.

"Memory is a form of protection," he said. "We remember so we do not become smaller than what we survived."

That was enough.

Special care had been taken with two bodies.

Mama Bear was laid with tokens from across the zoo—branches, smooth stones, pieces of old enrichment toys, even a scrap of red fabric Tashi had carried since the day she found him. Eliza's mother rested beside her, wrapped not in ceremony but in purpose: Daniel's jacket folded carefully around her shoulders, her knife placed at her side.

Eliza stood between Daniel and Tashi, holding both their hands.

When the flames rose, she did not look away. Neither did Tashi.

Happy watched the fire in silence, trunk resting on the ground. He had learned that strength could build and destroy—but also that it could *hold*. He stayed near Eliza after that, not as a guard, but as something steadier.

Ira, perched nearby, murmured observations no one had asked for and everyone secretly needed. He had become the keeper of small truths: where supplies were hidden, which paths were safest, who needed checking on when the night grew quiet. He would never call himself important. No one else agreed.

Tucker paced along the perimeter, tail flicking, still spinning stories—some alarmist, some half-true—but even he had changed. He watched now. Verified. When danger came, his warnings landed closer to reality than they used to. The zoo tolerated him because the zoo had learned that even flawed voices had value when they were no longer allowed to rule alone.

Attenborough stood with the beavers, reviewing schematics scratched into the dirt. "It's not perfect," he said. It never needed to be.

When the fire burned low, Daniel knelt and pressed his palm to the ground.

"This place has changed," he said quietly. "It's no longer just a zoo."

Nej tilted his head.

"It's a home," he replied.

The animals gathered closer.

"Then we call it Manor Zoo," Daniel said. "Not because it belongs to us. But because we are responsible for it."

No one objected.

The sun rose over reinforced walls and quiet smoke. Inside them, life resumed—not as it had been, but as it needed to be.

And for the first time since the world fell apart, something new stood where fear had once ruled:

A place built not on power, but on protection.

A place that remembered.

A place that held.

Manor Zoo.

MANOR ZOO

About the Author

Writing this book was such an emotional roller coaster. Oddly enough, this book is the product of an overactive imagination. One day while doom-scrolling on my phone, watching way more videos than I meant to, I found one of the wonderful videos of zoo keepers being tormented in the most delightful way but the most playful pandas.

I started imagining a world where pandas could see humans in the wild and know that we were not a threat. I started to wonder how such a world could exist. I imagined that getting to that level of comfort around humans would require there to be a lot less humans, which turned my thoughts back to the pandemic. And I obviously imagined the pandemic taking a different turn than it did.

A zoo without humans brought to my mind George Orwell's classic political allegory, *Animal Farm.* I started imagining how animals would feel about humans after spending a life in the zoo. Would they trust humans after being taken care of for so long, or would they see humans as their captors? Or would animals revert to their instincts and see each other as predator or prey?

From there, my imagination just played. What animals would I use, and what would each animal stand for symbolically? Getting to know each of the characters and watch them grow and develop was such an emotional journey. I laughed when Ernie and Aslan reunited. I cried at countless deaths, and I cried even harder at the redemptive moments that allowed a character to be seen by others the way they see themselves, and I felt inspired as the line was drawn between tolerance and intolerance.

I am so grateful for the opportunity to write this book, and I couldn't have done it without the love and support of so many people. Rachael, my partner, whose generosity and compassion remind me every day that time is never wasted when spent in the service of others, I love you with all of my heart. To our children, Brady, Nevaeh, Hayden, and Sage, it was a shock to me when I discovered you within the pages of this book. Brady, you are Mowgli who would rather accept personal injury than complacency when you see someone in trouble. Nevaeh, whose limitless dedication to loving those who look up to you I see in Mama Bear, you are my hero. Hayden and Sage, you both are the Tashi and Eliza of my life. You both inject joy into everything you do, and I could not be more grateful for both of you.

There have been so many guiding lights for me, and I couldn't possibly list them all. The continued support of my BookTok family and readers. Thank you so much to each and every one of you.

For information about events, upcoming projects, and
links to existing works, check out
www.jamesmichaelwrites.com.

James Michael
Writes